Wagging
Through
the Snow

Books by Laurien Berenson

A PEDIGREE TO DIE FOR
UNDERDOG
DOG EAT DOG
HAIR OF THE DOG
WATCHDOG
HUSH PUPPY
UNLEASHED
ONCE BITTEN
HOT DOG
BEST IN SHOW
JINGLE BELL BARK
RAINING CATS AND DOGS
CHOW DOWN
HOUNDED TO DEATH
DOGGIE DAY CARE MURDER
GONE WITH THE WOOF
DEATH OF A DOG WHISPERER
THE BARK BEFORE CHRISTMAS
LIVE AND LET GROWL
MURDER AT THE PUPPY FEST
WAGGING THROUGH THE SNOW

Published by Kensington Publishing Corporation

Wagging Through the Snow

LAURIEN BERENSON

KENSINGTON BOOKS
www.kensingtonbooks.com

KENSINGTON BOOKS are published by

Kensington Publishing Corp.
119 West 40th Street
New York, NY 10018

All Kensington titles, imprints and distributed lines are available at special quantity discounts for bulk purchases for sales promotion, premiums, fund-raising, educational or institutional use. Special book excerpts or customized printings can also be created to fit specific needs. For details, write or phone the office of the Kensington Special Sales Manager: Kensington Publishing Corp., 119 West 40th Street, New York, NY, 10018. Attn. Special Sales Department. Phone: 1-800-221-2647.

Kensington and the K logo Reg. U.S. Pat. & TM Off.

Library of Congress Control Number: 2017944851

ISBN-13: 978-1-4967-1298-1
ISBN-10: 1-4967-1298-6
First Kensington Hardcover Edition: October 2017

eISBN-13: 978-1-4967-1300-1
eISBN-10: 1-4967-1300-1
First Kensington Electronic Edition: October 2017

10 9 8 7 6 5 4 3 2 1

Printed in the United States of America

Wagging
Through
the Snow

Chapter One

"Ho! Ho! Ho!"

I was sitting at the kitchen table, working on a project for one of my fellow teachers when the back door to the house flew open. A blast of frigid air hit my papers and sent them scattering across the tabletop. My hasty grab to save them didn't help. Instead, I knocked into my laptop and sent it spinning into my half-full coffee mug.

Five black Standard Poodles had been snoozing on the floor at my feet. Startled by the intrusion, they jumped up and began to bark. Bud, the little spotted mutt who was the latest addition to our canine pack, scuttled over to stand beneath my chair. Quickly I righted the mug and scrambled to gather the papers before they could blow off the table.

Peace and quiet to utter mayhem in under ten seconds. Even for my house, that was a record.

I turned and aimed a withering look at our uninvited guest. My brother, Frank, was standing in the open doorway, grinning like a fool. Unfortunately, that was nothing new.

"Some welcoming committee," he said, gazing at the dogs.

The Poodles were now looking embarrassed by their outburst. Of course they recognized Frank. They just hadn't expected him to come flying through the door on this tranquil Saturday morning.

Any more than I had.

"Be glad they didn't bite you," I told him.

"They wouldn't do that." Frank took a step back. "*Would they?*"

Nope. No way. Not unless they thought there was a dire need.

My dogs were Standard Poodles, the largest of the three Poodle varieties. They were smart, funny, perceptive, and wonderfully affectionate. Poodles are people dogs. They would definitely attempt to think their way through a problem before resorting to violence.

On the other hand, my little brother has often been the bane of my existence. Maybe it wasn't a bad thing he didn't realize that.

"Come inside and close the door," I said. "It's freezing out there."

"It's December," Frank told me. Like we weren't all aware. "Merry Christmas!"

"Oh please. Christmas is a month away. We're still eating leftover turkey from Thanksgiving."

Frank shut the door, then pulled off his parka and draped it over the back of a chair. "It's never too early to embrace the Christmas spirit."

He walked over to the counter, got a mug out of the cabinet, and poured himself some coffee. The Poodles had yet to resettle and were still milling around the room. Faith, the oldest of the group, was keeping an eye on Frank. As he made himself at home in my kitchen, she shot me a look. *Is that allowed?*

I nodded silently. Faith has been part of my life for nearly eight years. I had never had a pet as a child, so she'd introduced me to the joys of dog ownership. I'd immediately fallen in love with Faith's sweet disposition, her empathetic nature, and her goofy sense of humor. My Poodle and I are soul mates. The relationship we share is deeper and more meaningful than I ever imagined was possible.

Faith found a quiet spot on the floor to lie down. I pushed my work stuff aside as my brother sank into a chair on the other side of the table. It looked like he was going to be here awhile.

"Is there any particular reason why we're feeling the need to embrace Christmas already?" I asked.

"As it happens, there is." Frank made a show of looking around the room. "Where is everyone?"

Aside from the six dogs who were very much in evidence, the rest of the family included my husband, Sam, our three-and-a-half-year-old son, Kevin, and Davey, our older son from my first marriage. On weekend mornings, our house is usually a hub of activity. I should have known better than to think I would actually score an uninterrupted hour in which to get some work done.

"Davey spent the night with Bob and Claire." Bob was my ex-husband and Claire was his new wife. Married the previous New Year's Eve, they lived in a house on the other side of Stamford. "He'll be back this afternoon. Sam and Kev are running errands."

I looked pointedly at the cluttered tabletop. "I'm supposed to be working."

Frank leaned forward eagerly. His straight brown hair, the same tawny shade as my own, fell forward over his eyes. Absently, he reached up and brushed it back. My brother and I also shared hazel eyes and a strong, determined, chin—a feature that looked better on him than me.

Beyond the physical similarities, however, Frank and I didn't have a lot in common. Growing up with a four-year age difference, we were always more likely to be squabbling than to have each other's backs. Even now that we're in our thirties—with Frank married to one of my best friends and partner in a thriving business—I still find it hard to think of my little brother as a mature adult.

"What are you working on?" he asked.

"Just school stuff."

"Like what?"

See, this is the problem. I'm pretty sure that Frank didn't show up in my kitchen at ten o'clock on a snowy weekend morning to talk about my job. For the record, I work as special needs tutor at a private academy in Greenwich, Connecticut. Frank is already well aware of that. Which means that for some reason he's either stalling or trying to butter me up.

Color me skeptical, but neither of those options ever seems to end well. For me, that is. Things often turn out just fine for Frank.

But since I wasn't in any hurry to find out what sort of dilemma he'd found himself in now, I figured I might as well humor him. "Remember the Christmas bazaar last year at Howard Academy?"

"Who could forget it?" Frank smirked. "You were in charge of running the event and your Santa Claus got himself killed."

"Most people wouldn't find that funny," I told him.

"Most people don't have a sister who has a habit of tripping over dead bodies."

Sadly, he did have a point.

"It turns out that Russell Hanover, HA's headmaster, has asked me not to participate in this year's bazaar."

"Gee, I wonder why."

I ignored him and said, "I'm organizing my notes so I can hand them over to the new chairman, in case he wants to see what worked for me and what didn't."

"Big help, Mel. I'm pretty sure he already knows what didn't work." Frank was laughing now.

It was almost enough to make me wish one of the Poodles *had* bitten him. Maybe Tar. He's our older male Standard, a retired specials dog who'd enjoyed an enviable career in the dog show ring. Tar is drop-dead gorgeous. He's also endearing, endlessly amusing, and, well . . . dumb. Tar is the only Poodle I've ever met who's lacking in intelligence. He makes up for that deficiency by trying really hard to get things right.

Tar *wants* to be good. He just doesn't always succeed. And usually he hasn't a clue why. Come to think of it, he and Frank had more than a little in common.

"Very funny," I said. It was time to cut to the chase. "Frank, why are you here?"

"About that. . . ." He gazed at me earnestly across the table. "I need a favor."

Quelle surprise.

Then a sudden thought hit me. "Is everything all right at home? Bertie's doing well? Maggie and Josh are fine?"

Bertie and I had been friends for almost a decade, She'd been married to my brother for half that time.

Their daughter, Maggie, was four and their second child, a son named Josh, had been born in September. The pregnancy wasn't an easy one and ten weeks after Josh's arrival, Bertie was still taking time to regain her footing.

"Sure, they're great. Bertie and Mags have everything under control. It's just that Josh, well, he's . . ."

"A baby?"

Frank winced. "I guess I didn't remember this part. Josh cries a lot. I mean, he really wails. Maggie never did that."

"Maggie wasn't colicky," I told him. "You know Bertie had Josh checked out and he's fine. This is just a stage he's going through."

"Yes, but that doesn't make it any easier. I feel like I haven't slept in days."

If Frank was angling for sympathy, he wasn't going to find it here. "Poor you," I said. "Does Bertie need my help?"

"Bertie?" Frank frowned. "Why are we talking about her? *I'm* the one with a problem."

Of course he was. I should have realized that. I settled back in my chair and asked, "What did you do now?"

"It wasn't my fault."

It never is, I thought with a sigh.

"You know The Bean Counter's been doing great, right?"

I nodded.

The Bean Counter was a café situated just north of the Merritt Parkway in Stamford. Originally opened by Frank, the bistro was now owned and operated in partnership with my ex-husband, Bob. The two men worked well together. Frank served as manager while Bob took care of the finances. Over the years, the café's popularity had grown and now it was considered a trendy destination for people who lived and worked in the area.

"Things are going so well that Bob decided we should start looking around at other investments," Frank explained. "Mostly real estate, because here in Fairfield County it's hard to go wrong."

"That sounds like a good idea," I said cautiously.

"I know, right?"

Frank sounded so eager for my approval that I found myself nodding again.

"So here's what happened. Yesterday morning, Josh *would not* stop crying. It was making me crazy. I had to get away, you know? So I figured I'd hop in the car and go for a drive."

It might have been more helpful if he'd taken Josh for a drive, I thought. Apparently that useful idea hadn't occurred to my brother.

"So there I was meandering around Wilton, not going anywhere in particular, when I saw a sign by the side of the road. It said ABSOLUTE AUCTION! ALL

BIDS ACCEPTED! It turned out that ten acres of land was being sold to settle an estate. And just my luck, the auction was taking place at noon. I figured I might as well go have a look."

Oh boy. I could guess where this story was heading. Frank never had been able to resist a deal.

"Only a couple of other guys even showed up to bid. Maybe because it was the day after Thanksgiving, and everyone else was busy at the mall. Honest to God, I was only planning to watch and see how it went. But . . ."

"You raised your hand, didn't you?"

"I had to," Frank said earnestly. "Compared to the other lots Bob and I had looked at, this place was a *steal*. Ten acres of forested land in the northeast corner of Wilton. Wait 'til you see it."

I didn't need to see the property to know that if a deal sounded too good to be true, there had to be a catch.

"You know there's probably something wrong with it," I said. "Some zoning issue or easement dispute that needs to be resolved. Maybe the place is all wetlands. And an absolute auction means you own that land now, no matter what the problem is."

"I'm not worried about that." Frank brushed off my concern. "I'm sure Bob will get everything straightened out."

Possibly, I thought, depending on what the difficulty was. But Frank might also be placing too much faith in his partner's abilities. Bob was an accountant, not a magician.

"I'm glad you're happy with your purchase," I told him. "But there's really no need for me to see it."

"Sure there is! You haven't even heard the best part yet."

"There's more?" I asked dubiously.

"This isn't just any old piece of land with trees on it. The old guy who owned the place died over the summer, but through last winter he was running a seasonal business there. You're going to love this. Our new property is a Christmas tree farm!"

It took me a minute to form a suitable reply.

Frank couldn't wait that long. "Isn't it great?" he prompted.

"Um . . . yes?"

"And Christmas is in four weeks. Which makes this whole thing, like, perfect."

No. It was so not *like, perfect*.

"Frank, what are you going to do with a Christmas tree farm?"

"Get it up and running, of course."

"Don't you have to make preparations to do something like that?"

Frank, never one to plan ahead, seemed surprised by the question. "Like what?"

I could think of half-a-dozen answers off the top of

my head. I went for the most obvious one. "Maybe grow some trees?"

"That's the beauty of it. The place is already overgrown. It's a veritable wilderness out there." My brother refused to let my misgivings dampen his enthusiasm. "You'll see. That land is going to pay us back in no time."

His phrasing brought me up short.

"Just to be clear," I said. "By *us*, you mean you and Bob, right? Sam and I aren't any part of this scheme."

"Not unless you want to be. But if I were you, I wouldn't make any hasty decisions about that. Wait until you see the place."

At least that was good to know. I was still feeling suspicious, however.

I peered at my brother across the table. "Have we come to the part yet where you ask me for a favor?"

"It's about Bob."

There was a sudden, sinking feeling in my stomach. "You talked to him before buying this place, didn't you?"

"Not exactly," Frank admitted. "Because I never meant to bid. And then it all happened so fast there wasn't time to check with him."

That was bad. Possibly really bad.

"You and Bob are supposed to be partners," I said. "And he has no idea you spent his investment money on a Christmas tree farm?"

"It's my money too." Frank sounded defensive. "And I know he'll be fine with the idea once he has a chance to think about it. That's where you come in. You guys are still friends even though you're not married anymore. I figured you could break the news to him."

Chapter
Two

I shot that idea down in a hurry. Then for my second act, I ushered my brother firmly out the door. After that, I went back to work. That lasted approximately twenty minutes before all you-know-what broke loose again. At least this time the chaos involved people I was happy to see.

"We got kibble!" Kevin announced. Almost four, he has yet to learn how to use his indoor voice. Or maybe he was just trying to make himself heard from within the pack of Poodles—including honorary member Bud—that was now eddying around his short legs.

"Forty pounds." Sam followed Kev through the connecting door from the garage, cradling the first bag in his arms. "That should last us a while."

Sam is tall, and strong, and surprisingly graceful. He has a great smile and the hands of a virtuoso. When he yanked off his wool cap and tossed it on the counter his blond hair, currently cropped short, stood straight up. If he hadn't been carrying twenty pounds of dog food, I'd have reached up and smoothed it back into place. As it was, I jumped up and hurried to open the pantry door.

Inside, the bag landed on the floor with a loud thump. Sam emerged from the pantry and headed back to the garage for the second load. I started to follow, then realized that Kev was peeling off his mittens and down jacket. He dropped them on the floor, then sat down to yank off his red rubber boots.

I quickly nudged aside the Poodles and scooped up Kev's discarded clothing before Bud could beat me to it. That little dog was obsessed with knitwear. Winter had barely begun and we were already on our third pair of mittens.

"Boots and jacket in the closet," I said to Kevin, handing them over.

He ambled toward the front hall and a Poodle escort followed. Kevin has been known to drop cookies, shoes, and the occasional rawhide strip. Tar, Faith's daughter, Eve, and our younger male, Augie, trailed along behind him, no doubt hoping for edible discards.

Bud, meanwhile, had given up on the mittens and gone trotting into the pantry. He was probably checking out the new bag of kibble. Half-starved when he'd been dumped by the side of the road the previous summer, the small dog had gained back all the weight he needed and more. Pretty soon he was going to be on a diet.

"Anything exciting happen while we were gone?" Sam asked when he'd delivered the second bag, shooed Bud out of the pantry, and firmly shut the door behind him.

The question—Sam's customary homecoming query—had become a standing joke. The way my life went, you'd think he would know better than to ask. But apparently not.

"Frank dropped by," I said.

"Just Frank? Not Bertie and the kids? Is everything all right?"

"More or less. My brother made an impulse purchase yesterday. He stopped in to tell me about it."

Sam had crouched down beside our fifth Standard Poodle, Raven. He was ruffling his hands through her coat. "Christmas shopping already? Good for Frank. If he braved the mall on the day after Thanksgiving, he's a better man than I am."

"He didn't go to the mall." I pulled out my chair and sat back down. "Frank bought a Christmas tree farm."

Sam paused to let that sink in. Then he looked up. "You're kidding, right?"

It took ten minutes to tell the whole story. Mostly because Sam alternated between interrupting me for details and laughing so hard that he couldn't hear what I was saying. By the time I was finished, he was shaking his head.

"So did you talk to Bob?"

"No way. Frank's going to have to break the news to Bob himself. I'm staying out of it."

Sam didn't look convinced. "Don't forget, Bob will be coming by later to drop off Davey. Frank's probably counting on you to tell him then."

"Then he's going to be disappointed," I said. "I've spent half my life cleaning up after my little brother. This time he's on his own."

Brave words. I just hoped I could make the resolution stick.

But as it turned out, I needn't have worried. The first thing Bob said upon his arrival was, "Did you hear what your harebrained brother has done now?"

"Hello to you too." I stepped around my ex-husband and gave Davey a quick hug.

Father and son, Bob and Davey were mirror images of one another. Both had sandy colored hair and dark eyes. They also shared the same lean, lanky build. At thirteen, Davey had yet to grow into the length of his limbs. Looking at him standing beside his father, I wondered if he ever would.

Davey gave me two seconds of hug-time, then squirmed out of my grasp. He tossed his backpack onto a nearby bench and said, "What's for dinner?"

"Guess."

"Not turkey again."

"You like turkey."

"Yeah, but not every day."

"Excuse me." Bob inserted himself between us. "Can we get back to what's important here? Your brother—"

"Your business partner," I corrected.

"—has bought himself a Christmas tree farm. What was he *thinking*?"

Davey had been on his way to the kitchen, but that pronouncement stopped him in his tracks. He spun around and stared at the two of us. "A Christmas tree farm? For real? Way to go, Frank!"

Someone growled under his breath. It might have been Bob.

I shooed Davey on his way and turned back to my ex-husband. "Apparently Frank was thinking that the two of you should open a new business selling trees."

Bob looked pained. "It's only four weeks until Christmas."

"Then you'd better hurry up and get started. Have you had a chance to take a look at the new property yet?"

Bob pushed aside Davey's backpack and sank down onto the wooden bench. "All I've seen so far are the few pictures the auction company put online to entice people to come to the sale. Although why anyone would be tempted by what they showed, I have no idea. The place looks pretty run-down. And that's putting it mildly."

"Frank told me that the owner passed away last summer," I said.

"Trust me, that place has been in a state of disrepair for a lot longer than that. Abel Haney was in his nineties when he died. He'd owned the land for fifty years and it doesn't look as though he'd made a single recent improvement. Who knows if the place is even compliant with current safety standards?"

"Abel Haney?" Sam came walking into the front hall. He was staring down at his phone. "As in Haney's Holiday Home? It says here that your Christmas tree farm has been a seasonal fixture in North Wilton for decades. *Fairfield County Magazine* even named it a 'top holiday attraction.'"

"I'll bet," Bob muttered. "What year was that?"

Sam squinted at the screen. "Nineteen eighty-eight."

"That's a whole different century." Davey laughed from the kitchen doorway. "I wasn't even born then."

"That Frank, he's a dreamer," I said happily. Wasn't it wonderful that this wasn't my problem?

"That's one way of putting it." Bob clearly wasn't amused. "Don't think I'm forgetting it was your fault that I went into business with your brother in the first place."

"Oh no you don't," I said. "You are not blaming

this problem on me. Besides, until yesterday the two of you made great partners. Look at The Bean Counter. It's a big success."

"And do you know why?" Bob shot back. "Because each of us has stuck to doing what we're good at. Frank is operations and I'm finance. He's not supposed to wake up one morning and decide to squander *my* money on some holiday pipe dream."

Sam cleared his throat. "It wasn't entirely your money, was it?"

"Like that makes all the difference." Bob braced his hands on either side of the oak bench and pushed himself to his feet. "I suppose there's no point in complaining about something I can't change. The only thing left to do now is go have a look at the place, and see what we've gotten ourselves into." He pulled the edges of his parka together and ran up the zipper. "How's tomorrow? Are you guys free?"

Sam, Davey, and I shared a look.

"What?" Bob stared at the three of us. "Of course you're coming. I'm not checking out Haney's Holiday Home on my own."

"Now that you own the place, it needs a new name," Davey said. "What about Frank's Folly?"

"You're not helping." I pointed toward the kitchen where Davey was supposed to be doing something. Anything. I didn't even care what. He eluded my outstretched hand with a grin.

"Call it whatever you like, but you guys are in on

this too," Bob said. "Eleven o'clock. I'll see you there."

Sam watched as Bob left, pulling the door shut behind him. "That must be why you divorced that man," he said thoughtfully.

"What do you mean?"

"You've never been good at taking orders."

I wanted to muster some outrage at that, but I really couldn't. Whatever.

Early Sunday morning my phone rang. A glance at the name on the screen confirmed what I'd already suspected. The only surprise was that it had taken her this long.

Even in a family as contentious as mine, Aunt Peg was notable for her forceful personality, her unending curiosity, and her total inability to ever, under any circumstances, *leave well enough alone*. Which meant that if there was trouble brewing anywhere in the vicinity, Aunt Peg wanted in. And if possible, she'd also like to drag her relatives into the fray too.

So this situation had the potential to be the sum of all good things as far as she was concerned. Christmas. Family troubles. And Bob had a problem. Did I mention that Aunt Peg and my ex-husband don't get along? To say that she would greet his tree farm predicament with gusto was an understatement. I could practically picture her rubbing her hands together with glee.

"I take it you've heard the news," I said into the phone.

"Claire called me," Aunt Peg replied. "Thank goodness I have *one* relative who takes the time to keep me informed."

Claire was a relatively new addition to the family. She was still naïve enough to believe that Aunt Peg used her formidable powers for better, rather than worse. She'd learn.

"I hear you're going to have a look at the place."

"So Bob tells me," I said. "It didn't sound like we had a choice."

"Excellent. Eleven o'clock, right? I'll see you there."

She disconnected before I even had a chance to ask if she'd been invited to accompany us. Which was obviously a moot point. But still.

Faith and Eve were lying on the nearby bed. Both their heads had been inquisitively cocked to one side as I'd spoken on the phone. Two sets of dark eyes watched as I put the device down on my dresser. I was certain they knew who I'd been talking to.

Aunt Peg was a renowned Standard Poodle breeder. She was also a long-time dog show exhibitor and now a Toy and Non-Sporting group judge. Her Cedar Crest Kennel had produced many of the best Standard Poodles bred and shown in the U.S. Dogs were Aunt Peg's vocation and her passion. And no matter how often she and I clashed, I would always be grateful for the fact that Faith had entered my life as a gift from Aunt Peg.

There was no way I could ever repay her for that and we both knew it.

"I'm sorry," I told the two Poodles. "She didn't ask to talk to you."

It was clear they didn't believe me.

"Really," I said. "Would I lie to you?"

Eve hopped down off the bed and left the room. Davey appeared in the doorway a moment later. He was wearing flannel-lined jeans, Bean boots, and a thick Williams College sweatshirt: warm clothes for tramping around a snowy tree farm.

"Blueberry pancakes for breakfast," he told me. "Sam's cooking. If you don't hurry up, Kev and I will eat them all before you get there."

He didn't have to tell me twice.

Chapter
Three

From our house in Stamford, the drive to north-west Wilton took twenty-five minutes. Though it was only the last week of November, there was already snow on the ground. We'd had six inches on a school day two weeks earlier, followed by another three inches the day before Thanksgiving. New Englanders are used to dealing with winter weather, however, and even the small roads were clear and easily passable. It occurred to me as we neared our destination that a fresh coat of glistening snow might make the Christmas tree farm look more attractive than it otherwise would have.

Unfortunately, that turned out to be wishful thinking. My first impression of Frank's new acquisition was that it was hardly worth the trip.

Our only indication that we'd arrived at the right address was a faded wooden sign that had fallen off its post and was leaning against a tree by the side of the road. Block lettering that might have once been red, but was now a tacky shade of pink, announced the name of our destination. Beside the empty signpost, a narrow dirt driveway led the way into the densely wooded property. At least the driveway was plowed.

"Well." Sam cleared his throat as he nosed the SUV into the rutted lane. "This looks rustic."

Davey leaned toward his window for a better look. "I was going to say *shabby* myself."

The SUV bounced from side to side as we negotiated the driveway. I reached back to steady Kevin in his seat. "This is only the entrance. Maybe it will look better when we get to the buildings."

"Time to buy a Christmas tree?" Kev asked hopefully.

"Not today," I said. "We're just going to have a look around."

"Ornaments?"

"No ornaments," Davey told him. "But while the grown-ups are talking, you and I can collect pinecones. I bet we'll find lots of them around here."

Kevin clapped his hands. He enjoyed doing anything his big brother suggested.

A few seconds later, we emerged from the trees and got our first look at the portion of the property where Haney's Holiday Home conducted business. Sam lifted his foot off the gas pedal and the SUV rolled to a stop.

The driveway had been in a state of disrepair. What we saw before us looked even worse.

Two weathered clapboard buildings had been erected on the far side of a clearing. The smaller building had a corrugated roof and double garage doors. I guessed it was an equipment shed. Hopefully, it was only my imagination that the walls of the decrepit structure appeared to be swaying in the light breeze.

Thankfully, the larger structure looked more secure. A sign, stuck in the ground beside a shoveled walkway, identified that building as the office. Two wooden steps led to a covered porch whose banister was mostly intact. A narrow door, coated with peeling green paint, provided access to the building. It was flanked on either side by small, square windows whose glass was coated with grime.

A parking area on the other side of the clearing had recently been plowed, and I saw that we weren't the first to arrive. A black Jeep Wrangler was already pulled up beside a low drift. As Sam parked the SUV, the Wrangler's door opened and Frank hopped out.

"So . . ." he said, waving a hand expansively. "What do you think?"

I hoped to God he wasn't looking for an honest answer.

"It could do with some *sprucing* up," I told him.

Frank frowned. He didn't get it. "Well, sure. But

that's just cosmetic stuff. We can have that fixed in no time."

"Good one, Mom." Davey looked at me and grinned. That boy is a child after my own heart.

The sound of approaching cars had us all turning back to look at the tree-shrouded entrance. After a moment, Aunt Peg's minivan and Bob's dark green Explorer came bouncing into view.

"Your driveway needs some work," Sam commented.

"It's too late now, but we'll get to that next year," Frank told him. "I'll be sure to earmark some of the profits for paving."

"*Some of the profits?*" Sam muttered under his breath.

I looked at him and shrugged.

There'd been plenty of times in the past when Frank's optimism had left me feeling incredulous too. My brother has a tendency to leapfrog over problems, seeing only the desired solution that lies ahead. Sometimes that tunnel vision worked for him. Other times it left him knocked flat on his back and wondering where things had gone wrong.

Davey unloaded Kevin from the SUV. I took a minute to check that his boots were fastened and his mittens were actually on his hands. By the time that was done, Bob and Aunt Peg had parked and joined us.

We all stood and stared at the pair of dilapidated buildings.

"Hey," Frank said suddenly. "There's even a chimney. I bet the office has a fireplace."

I saw Bob's eyes widen fractionally. He turned and looked at his partner. "Don't you *know*?"

"Um . . . not exactly."

"But you must have gone inside the building before you bought it." When Frank didn't reply right away, Bob added, "You *did* look inside the building, didn't you?"

"I would have." Frank's voice edged toward a whine. "But the auction was hectic and there wasn't time."

"*No time to step inside a building that you were planning to buy?*"

"Land!" Frank blurted out. He sounded pleased with himself, as if he'd come up with a particularly clever answer. "I was buying the *land*. Look around. Isn't it beautiful?"

I had to admit, what we could see of the property did possess a certain pastoral charm. Particularly if you were willing to look past the tattered buildings and pothole-filled parking lot and fasten your gaze on the wondrous forest of pine trees that spread out around us in three directions. As I'd suspected it might, the blanket of new snow had freshened everything up. I hated to think what Haney's Holiday Home might look like during spring thaw.

Aunt Peg was already on her way to the steps.

"Rather than standing here wondering what's inside, let's go have a look, shall we?"

The porch sagged beneath our collective weight as Frank fished around in his pocket for the key to open the office door. While we waited, Bob stepped to one side and pulled out his phone. He began to record what sounded like a to-do list.

"Replace front step," I heard him say quietly. "Brace banister. Check porch supports."

Davey and Kevin had remained behind on the walk. Davey took his little brother's hand and said, "Kev and I are going to go explore the woods, okay?"

"I guess that's all right." I looked at Sam, who nodded. "But don't go too far. And don't get lost. And don't let Kevin out of your sight."

"*Mo-o-om.*" Davey stopped just short of rolling his eyes. "It's all good. We'll be fine. They're just trees."

"*Strange* trees," I clarified. Then frowned. Even to my own ears that sounded overly protective. "Don't get into any trouble. And if you do, come right back."

"No trouble," Kevin agreed. "We're going to look for pinecones."

"And grizzly bears," Davey told him.

Kev's mouth opened to form a round O.

"No bears," I said quickly. "No coyotes. No beavers. In fact, no wildlife at all. Got it?"

"Got it," Davey called back over his shoulder as he and his brother went tromping away through the snow.

"Got it!" Frank announced, pulling the key out of his pocket.

It was an ornate skeleton key, at least four inches in length. Bronze in color, it looked heavy. How Frank could have misplaced something that size in his pants pocket, I had no idea. He shoved the key in the lock and turned it hard to the right.

For a moment, nothing happened. Then we heard a small thud as the bolt receded. Frank turned the knob and pushed. The door didn't budge.

"Oil hinges," Bob said into his phone.

Frank turned the knob again. This time he applied his shoulder to the door and pushed harder. There was a sharp squeal as it finally gave way. The door swung open before us and revealed . . . virtually nothing.

The four of us stood on the porch and squinted into the building's dimly-lit interior. The only available light was that filtering through the dirty window-panes. The bright glare of the sun on snow behind us didn't help. It made the single room appear darker and gloomier.

Frank remained undaunted. "There must be a light switch," he said. Reaching inside, his hand fumbled around the doorframe. A few seconds later, we heard a sharp click. "Found it!"

Nothing happened.

"Turn on electricity," Bob said into his phone.

"Wash windows," I muttered under my breath.

Frank shot us both a look. "Is that really necessary?"

"I should think so," Bob replied. But when Frank continued to glare at him, he made a show of turning off the device and tucking it in his pocket.

While the rest of us stood there wondering what to do next, Aunt Peg was ever prepared. "I thought something like this might happen. I've got a lantern in my van. Be right back."

In no time at all she was leading the way into the building.

The interior room looked to be about twenty feet square. Shelves, now empty, lined one of the unfinished wooden walls. On the other side was a waist-high counter. An old-fashioned cash register sat on top of it. Its drawer was open and also empty. A cane and wooden rocking chair with a well-worn seat had been abandoned in one corner. Frank had been wrong about the fireplace, but there was a wood-burning stove. A box next to it held a pair of fire tongs and small pile of logs.

Dust motes, stirred up by our footsteps, danced in the stale air around us and I stifled the urge to sneeze. A long, vinyl banner lay curled up on the wood plank floor. Sam picked it up, spread it out on the counter, and read aloud, "After Christmas Sale! Everything Half Off! All Decorations Must Go!"

"It seems kind of sad." My eyes came to rest on the rocking chair. "When Mr. Haney closed up this building last January, he had no idea that he'd never be back."

"Perhaps not," Aunt Peg said tartly. "But he doesn't seem to have left much behind."

"Haney's loss is our gain." Never one to dwell on sentiment, Frank was walking around the room, checking things out. "This place has potential, doesn't it? Okay, so it needs to be cleaned up and aired out. But that's no big deal. Picture the room decorated with holly and pine boughs, and maybe some swags of red ribbon."

My brother's gaze flicked in Bob's direction. "Claire could be in charge. She's great with stuff like that."

Bob didn't even hesitate before shaking his head. "Before you go nominating my wife to be in charge of housekeeping—which, by the way, is something she won't thank you *or* me for—I think we need to discuss the feasibility of getting this business up and running at all. Is that something we even want to tackle? Especially on such short notice."

"Sure it is," Frank replied. "Haney's Holiday Home is a Christmas tradition. It was even profiled in a magazine. You told me Sam said so."

Sam held up his hands in a display of innocence. He wasn't about to assume credit or blame for any part of this project. "All I did was look it up on the internet. Anyone could have done that."

"Think of all the children whose holidays will be ruined if their families aren't able to come here like they've always done and cut down their own special Christmas tree," Frank implored.

"Heaven forbid they have to buy a tree from a nursery," I said.

"Or Walmart," Sam added. It looked like he was trying not to laugh.

"You see?" Frank said to Bob. "Haney's Holiday Home isn't just a business. It's a community service."

Aunt Peg leaned toward Frank and said in a stage whisper, "Don't oversell it. Back off now and give Bob a day or two to think about it. He'll come around."

"I will?" Bob sounded surprised.

"Of course," Aunt Peg told him. "Christmas is coming and you own a Christmas tree farm. If that isn't fate, I don't know what is."

We heard a clatter from outside. Davey came racing up the steps and through the open doorway.

"I thought I told you not to let go of your brother's hand," I said as he skidded to a stop.

"He's right behind me," Davey said breathlessly. Thank goodness he was right. "You guys better come and have a look. There's something weird out here."

"Weird how?" Aunt Peg immediately perked up. While the rest of us were processing that information, she was already on her way to the door.

Davey gulped for air. "Out in the woods. It sounds like someone's crying."

"You're imagining things," Frank said with a snort.

Davey looked at me and shook his head. *Damn.* I had hoped Frank was right.

We all scrambled through the doorway together. As Sam scooped Kevin up in his arms, I shut the door behind us. Davey flew across the porch and hopped down the two steps. "This way."

At first glance, the wooded area behind the building looked as though its trees had been planted in an orderly fashion. Although that might have been the case at one point, once we entered the forest it quickly became clear how overgrown the farm's cash crop had been allowed to become.

The main path leading into the woods was about six feet wide and clogged with snow. Foliage encroached on either side. Some of the Christmas trees were only waist-high. Others soared way above my head. Most appeared to be Scotch pine, but I also saw some spruces and a batch of balsam firs. Mr. Haney had clearly believed in catering to a variety of tastes.

Aunt Peg was out ahead of us. Moving with assurance, she was retracing the footsteps the boys had left in the almost knee-deep snow. Determined to catch up, I raced ahead of the rest of the group.

We left the main path behind and veered off into the trees. The vegetation was thicker there. Snow-covered boughs hung low over the narrow trail. I'd gone about fifty feet when the sound of a soft, mournful whimpering made me stop abruptly in my tracks.

"See?" Davey came up behind me. "I told you. Something's out there."

"Go back and take Kevin from Sam," I told him. "You two stay behind the adults while we go see what it is."

Reluctantly, Davey did as I'd requested. As soon he reached the three men I took off again, following in Aunt Peg's footsteps. In the quiet woods, the low, mewling sound seemed to float on the light breeze. It had an almost ghostly quality. I could feel the hair on the back of my neck beginning to rise.

It was hard to travel fast in the wet snow. I was looking down and watching where I was placing my feet, so when Aunt Peg stopped unexpectedly, I almost ran into her.

Aunt Peg is nearly six feet tall and broader than I am. There was no way I could see around her. As I ducked to one side, pushing several heavy branches out of my way, I heard her suck in a sharp breath.

Then the view in front of me cleared and I saw what she had seen.

The body of a man was lying in a drift of snow beneath a lush fir tree. There was a jagged, bloody gash across the top of his head. A thick branch, broken off the tree above, lay on the ground beside him. The man's skin was pale and waxy looking. His eyes were open and staring at the sky.

I flinched and quickly turned away. When I raised my hands and held them in place, Frank, Sam, Bob, and the boys halted immediately. No one needed to come any closer. There was nothing any of us could do to help.

Whatever had made the sound that drew us to this place, it was clear that we'd arrived too late.

Chapter
Four

Bob called the police. Sam hustled the kids back down the path and took them home. Under these gruesome circumstances, Aunt Peg definitely wouldn't be going anywhere. I knew I could catch a ride with her later.

My brother has never been the most useful person in an emergency. Now Frank walked into a nearby thicket of trees and threw up. As he finished heaving, I once again heard the soft keening sound that had drawn us to the clearing in the first place.

Aunt Peg and I shared a startled glance.

"That man looks dead," I said. "He *is* dead, right?"

"*He* is," Aunt Peg replied. "But maybe he's not alone."

Davey had said there was something weird going on out here. As I recalled those words, I found my thoughts scattering in all sorts of unwelcome directions. Even in broad daylight. Even though I was accompanied by two strong men—and Aunt Peg, who could probably take them both down in a brawl.

While I was envisioning malevolent forest spirits, Aunt Peg opted for a more practical approach. Giving the body a wide berth, she trod carefully around to the other side of the clearing. There she knelt down in the snow, removed one of her gloves, and held out her hand.

"What are you doing?" I asked.

"I think there's something burrowed underneath the body. A little animal of some kind. I can see a pair of dark eyes looking out at me."

I took a step back. "Well, don't ask it to come out here. What if it's a wolverine? Or a biting otter?"

Aunt Peg cast me a look. "You don't spend much time in nature, do you?"

"Not in the woods. Not in the middle of winter."

"Trust me, it's not a biting otter. I think it might be a little white dog." She turned her attention back to the task at hand, beckoning as she crooned, "Come on out, little guy. Nobody's going to hurt you. You must be very cold under there. Come to me and I'll take care of you."

Aunt Peg loved dogs completely. She could communicate with them on a level most people didn't even know existed. If there was a dog in the world who could resist her charms, I had yet to meet it.

I heard a rustling sound, followed by scratching

and scrambling. A black nose poked out from beneath the body. Then a dirty white head emerged. After a brief hesitation a small, raggedy dog with dark, button eyes crawled out of his hiding place. He walked cautiously across the crusted snow to Aunt Peg's outstretched hand.

Even from afar, I could see that the bedraggled canine was wet and shivering.

Aunt Peg remained still as the dog sniffed her fingers. When he relaxed and pressed his head into her hand, she picked him up and tucked him against her body. "You poor thing. Have you been out here all night?"

"Possibly longer." I glanced at the corpse between us.

"The police are on their way," Bob said, returning to my side. "I sent Frank back to the office to wait for them. When they arrive, he'll show them where we are."

"Good idea." I was sure Frank had been grateful for the assignment.

Bob nodded in Aunt Peg's direction. "What's that?"

"Unless I miss my guess, it's a Maltese," she informed him.

A Maltese. There was a dead body lying on the ground just a few feet away. Somehow, that wasn't enough of a distraction to keep Aunt Peg from identifying the breed of the dog she held cradled in her arms. Amazing.

Bob looked around the clearing. "Where did it come from?"

"It was under the body," I told him. "It must have belonged to that man."

"He was keeping him company." Aunt Peg unzipped her parka and slipped the small dog inside, then closed her jacket again for warmth. "I suspect he was waiting for his owner to wake up."

We'd all been avoiding looking at the body. Now our attention was directed back that way.

"Who do you suppose he is?" asked Bob.

Aunt Peg took a step toward the corpse. "Maybe there's some ID in his coat."

"No. Don't." To my surprise, she stopped when I held up my hand. "You've already appropriated the guy's dog. I think we'd better let the police handle the rest."

"I guess you have a point." Aunt Peg gazed up at the tree above him. "That branch must have broken off and hit him on the head. But what do you suppose was he doing out here in the first place?"

"Walking his dog?" I said.

Bob frowned. "This is private property. The least he could have done was have the decency to die somewhere else."

In the silence that followed that statement, I could hear the sound of approaching sirens. It sounded as though the emergency crews had turned out in force. Wilton was a quiet town. I was guessing the police here didn't receive many reports of unidentified dead bodies.

"That's odd." Bob was still peering at the body on the ground.

"What is?" I asked.

"Look at the guy's clothes. He's got on a ton of layers to stay warm, but everything he's wearing looks old and worn. Even his boots."

I took a peek at the dead man's feet. There was a hole in one of his upturned soles and the toe of his other boot had been mended with duct tape.

"See what I mean?" Bob asked. "This is a nice area. If he lived around here—close enough to be out for a stroll in these woods—you'd think he wouldn't be wearing clothes that looked like they came from the Salvation Army. Or the dump."

"Maybe he's an eccentric recluse." Aunt Peg sounded pleased by the thought. "Or a hobo that hopped off a passing train."

Except there were no passing trains in the vicinity. As Aunt Peg knew perfectly well.

"Just my luck," Bob muttered. "I *knew* there had to be something sketchy about this deal. 'It's just beautiful open land and trees', Frank said. 'Undeveloped property in Wilton. What could possibly go wrong?' And here we are."

I'd expected there would be a catch too. But even I hadn't imagined one of this magnitude.

"I'm sure the police will get everything sorted out," I told him. "They'll remove the body and notify the next of kin. In an hour or two, this unfortunate episode will all be over and your life can go back to normal."

"Normal." Bob shook his head. "Which I suppose means going back to arguing with Frank about opening a Christmas shop on five minutes' notice."

The next hour passed in a flurry of activity. A pair of policemen were the first to arrive. They were followed by an ambulance and EMTs. The medical examiner rolled in after that. Frank kept busy making trips back and forth from the parking lot, directing each new group to the scene. Bob, who'd identified himself as co-owner of the property, was asked a multitude of questions—most of which he had no answers for.

Aunt Peg and I stood off to one side, trying to stay out of the way as the officers photographed the body, then conducted a brief examination. Mostly that seemed to consist of them pointing at the dead man's head wound, then at the broken tree branch, and nodding in agreement.

The police also searched the body for identification, but I didn't see them remove anything from the man's pockets. So when the officers stood up and stepped away from the body, I was surprised to overhear one of them refer to the man on the ground as Pete.

"Excuse me," I said to the one nearest me. "Do you know who that man is?"

Earlier, Aunt Peg and I had been asked to supply our names and the reason for our presence. The two policemen—busy dealing with Bob—hadn't bothered to introduce themselves to us. In the intervening time they'd neither paid us any further attention, nor commented on the little white dog whose head was clearly visible poking out of the opening of Aunt Peg's parka. Now they seemed surprised to hear me speak at all.

"His name is Pete," the officer replied.

Thanks to my big ears, I already knew that much. "Does he have a last name?"

"I'm sure he does, but I'm not aware of it."

"But you do recognize him?"

"We've seen him around town," the other policeman told me. "Pete's made his home in Wilton for quite a while now. Four or five years, I'd guess. Usually we'd see more of him in the summer months."

"Did he live around here?" I asked.

"That's the thing. Pete didn't live any one place in particular. He did quite a bit of wandering. Then he'd just set up camp wherever he found a likely spot."

"Are you saying that Mr. Pete here was homeless?" Aunt Peg asked.

"That's about the gist of it. People felt sorry for him and gave him money, most of which he took directly to the liquor store."

The first policeman added, "Pete didn't seem to have anywhere to go. And sometimes he got confused about where he was. But other than that, he was harmless. We made sure that he stayed away from the schools, but beyond that there wasn't much else we could do."

"But—" I sputtered. "Wasn't there a shelter he could go to? Some place safe that would take him in?"

"There are social services that could have helped him. But Pete would have had to do his part too. For one thing, he would have needed to get the drinking under control. For another, he had to want to be helped. Have you ever dealt with the homeless, ma'am?"

I shook my head.

"Many of them don't want to be part of the system. They prefer to make their own choices and look out for themselves. For some, that kind of enforced structure is something they purposely left behind. They'd rather live on the streets and maintain their independence. During the time Pete was here in Wilton, he always seemed to manage tolerably well."

"Until now," Aunt Peg said drily.

"Yes, ma'am," the officer agreed. "Until now."

He stepped away from us and walked over to confer with the EMTs. The medical examiner had arrived a few minutes earlier and the group of men stood huddled around the body. They spoke quietly among themselves, their voices too soft for me to hear what they were saying.

"What about Pete's dog?" I asked the officer who'd remained with us. "What will happen to him?"

"Dog?" His gaze shifted to Aunt Peg, who was frowning at me mightily. I could see that she was tempted to stuff the little Maltese down out of sight and zip the parka up to her chin. "Is that Snowball in there?"

"Snowball?"

"That's what Pete called him. He and that little dog were just about inseparable. Where'd you find him?"

"He was with the body, shivering and crying," Aunt Peg said. "That's how we came to find his owner."

The policeman frowned. "I suppose this means we'll have to call animal control. Of course, nobody's going to pick up that phone on the Sunday after Thanksgiving. And I suppose we can't leave him here. . . ."

"Certainly not," Aunt Peg said sharply. With effort, she moderated her tone. "If I may offer a solution. Why don't I take Snowball home with me until you're able to make other arrangements for his care? I assume you'll also be contacting Pete's next of kin?"

"We will do so if we're able to," he replied. "Right now, I wouldn't say that's a given. Pete's fingerprints might or might not be in the system. And we can check with social services to see what kind of information they have on him in their records. But we may have trouble making a positive ID."

"Surely his family will want to know what happened to him," I said.

"If he *has* family. Or any people at all who still care

about his welfare. I wouldn't say that's a given either. If you'll excuse me?" The officer left us and went to join the group of men beneath the tree.

Bob came over to stand beside us. Even though we'd been divorced for a dozen years, I could still read his moods. Now, for some reason, he looked relieved.

"They're saying there's no indication of foul play," he told us. "The guy appears to have frozen to death in the snow. Apparently he was known around here as a vagrant and an alcoholic. One of the EMTs said the body reeked of gin."

"What about the gash on his head?" I asked.

"They're guessing he was drunk, lost his balance, and grabbed the branch to steady himself. That— added to the weight of the snow on top of it—made the branch break and hit him on the head. The ME will do an autopsy, but he's pretty sure that once the guy was unconscious he died of exposure. It looks like it was just an unfortunate accident. So that's good news."

I turned and stared at him.

Bob's nose was already red from the cold. Now his cheeks grew red to match. "Sorry, I didn't mean that the way it sounded."

"I should hope not," said Aunt Peg. "But surely that can't be the whole story."

"Why not?" asked Bob. "It sounded logical to me."

"Didn't anybody stop to wonder why a homeless

man would have been way out here in the middle of nowhere, wandering around in the snow?"

"I didn't hear them say anything about that." Bob looked pained. He wanted answers, not more questions.

"That's what I was afraid of," Aunt Peg said.

Chapter
Five

Frank joined our small group and we withdrew to the head of the path. The authorities were wrapping things up.

Once they'd realized who the body in the snow belonged to, it felt as though the mood in the clearing had changed. Any sense of urgency had vanished. Now the authorities' response felt perfunctory.

It was as if the death of a homeless man was less important than the other things I could hear them discussing: an upcoming football game, a traffic accident on Route 7, their holiday vacation schedules. Dealing with the remains of the man we knew only as Pete was just another chore they needed to finish before moving on with the rest of their day.

"That was a good question," Bob said to Aunt Peg. He didn't look nearly as reassured as he had a few minutes earlier.

"Of course it was." She lowered her zipper a few inches, shifted the bundle beneath her parka from side to side, then looked pointedly at me. "Someone should try and figure out the answer."

"What question?" asked Frank.

"Aunt Peg wanted to know why a homeless man would have been out in these woods on a snowy winter night," I said.

"Hmm." Frank considered that. "I wonder if Sean Haney knows anything about him."

We all turned to look at him. Even Snowball popped his head out of the opening at the top of Aunt Peg's jacket.

"Who is Sean Haney and why might he know something?" she inquired.

"He's the former owner's son. I met him the other day at the auction. At the end of the bidding, he came over and shook my hand, and wished me luck with the property. Sean gave me his card, although at the time I couldn't imagine what I'd ever need it for. I think I tossed it in my glove compartment."

We made our way back down the now well-trampled trail. The small parking area was crowded with official vehicles. Frank skirted around them and went to his Jeep. He searched around the car for at least five minutes, but finally emerged holding a lavender-tinted business card.

"What does Sean Haney do?" Bob gazed at the

card with a slight smile on his face as Frank tapped out the number on his phone.

"According to this, he's the owner of Sean's Spa and Salon in Weston." My brother glanced up. "That family loves their alliteration, don't they?"

Frank put the phone to his ear, then walked several feet away so he could conduct the call in private. I wasn't having any of that. Bob and Aunt Peg hung back, but I shadowed his steps across the parking lot. I listened as my brother identified himself to Sean and explained what had happened.

Then there was a long period of silence, while Frank listened and frowned. "I see," he said.

"See what?" I mouthed impatiently.

Frank glared at me and angled his body away.

The evasive move annoyed me every bit as much as he'd known it would. Given the slightest opportunity, my brother and I snap right back into the fractious relationship we'd had as children.

"I see," Frank said again.

I walked around and planted myself in front of him. *Would it kill him to ask a pertinent question or two?*

"Uh-huh." Frank nodded. "I get that." He looked at me and stuck out his tongue.

And there it was. The last straw.

"Give me that." I reached over and snatched the phone out of Frank's hand. "Hello, Sean, this is Melanie Travis. I'm Frank's sister and I'm delighted that you have some information for us."

"Oh, I don't know about that," Sean replied. "But I'm happy to try to help if I can. I was just telling Frank a little bit about my day spa over here in Weston."

Seriously? They'd been talking for several minutes. Thank goodness I had appropriated the phone when I did.

"We offer the best massage therapy in all of Fairfield County," Sean continued happily. "And our mud and avocado wrap is second to none."

Clearly he was a guy who liked to talk. I hoped Sean would feel the same way after a change of subject.

"That sounds wonderful," I said. "But about the man whose body was found here this morning . . . the police told us his name was Pete."

"Yeah, Pete—that's it. I remember him."

"What do you know about him?"

"Truthfully, not a whole lot. The tree farm was my dad's thing, not mine. I haven't spent much time there in years. But Dad used to talk about some spacey dude who hung around the property in the winter. He was always trying to get the guy to stay out of sight during the holidays. Dad didn't want him interfering with customers who were in the woods chopping down Christmas trees."

"If Pete was a problem, why didn't your father tell him to leave?" I asked.

"Dad would never have done that. Pete was okay, just a little too into the sauce, if you know what I mean. Dad believed in paying things forward. He thought Pete was the kind of guy who could use a helping hand."

"Your father sounds like a lovely man," I said.

"He was," Sean agreed. "He was a practical man too. After the holiday season ended the farm just sat empty for the rest of the winter. Come spring, Dad could book events there, or sometimes commercial shoots. But January through March, the place was just a bunch of trees growing. So if Pete wanted to make his home in the woods for the winter, Dad wasn't about to object."

I tried unsuccessfully to picture how that would work. "Was Pete camping out there?"

"Oh, heck no." Sean laughed. "He'd have frozen if he did that. In the back of the property there's an old tumbledown shack. Been there for years. It's hardly much more than a roof, four walls, and a floor, but with a little stove I guess it stays warm enough."

"That sounds pretty Spartan."

"Tell me about it. I'm much too sociable to live like that, but Pete did okay. Dad always said it suited Pete, because the only thing he wanted was for the world to go away and leave him alone."

I exhaled slowly. "What a sad way to live. Did your father know why Pete felt that way?"

"If he did, he never told me. Tell the truth, I don't think Dad spent any time worrying about it. He just accepted Pete for who he was. If I had to hazard a guess, I'd say the drinking had something to do with it. And now your brother told me the police think that's what caused his death?"

"That's right," I said. "Did your father know Pete's last name? Or where he'd lived before he came to Wilton?"

"Stuff like that, Pete didn't talk about it and Dad didn't ask. That's probably why the guy kept coming back. Every year when the weather got warm again he'd disappear for a while. Probably found somewhere to hang out that better suited his needs. But he always seemed to find his way back to the farm in the fall."

"What about Pete's dog?" I asked.

"That little rug rat that followed him around? What about it?"

"Apparently it's a purebred Maltese. Do you know where it came from?"

"You're kidding me, right?" Sean snorted. "I don't even know what a purebred Maltese is, much less where you'd find one."

Okay, I'd been grasping at straws with that last question. But Aunt Peg would have been disappointed if I hadn't at least tried.

"Thank you for taking the time to talk to us," I said. "You've given us more information than we had."

"So?" Aunt Peg demanded as I handed the phone back to Frank. While I'd been busy talking to Sean, she'd sidled over to stand beside me. "What does the younger Haney have to say for himself?"

Aunt Peg would want hard facts. Unfortunately, I had none to offer.

"That his day spa offers the best mud and avocado wrap around?"

"Mud and avocado," she sniffed. "That sounds disgusting. What else?"

"He didn't have much information about Pete," I admitted. "But he did point us in the right direction."

"Excellent," said Aunt Peg. "Which way?"

"North." I pointed. "Into the woods."

Frank and Bob both declined to participate in an excursion back into the forest to look for Pete's cabin. Aunt Peg and I were fine with that. Those two would only slow us down anyway.

We deliberately skirted around the clearing where Pete's body had recently lain. While we were in the parking lot, the authorities had transported the corpse out of the woods and placed it in the medical examiner's van. Shortly thereafter, the EMTs had been the first to depart. The police officers had paused to have a few words with Bob, then their cruiser and the ME's van had driven away as well. They were followed by Frank and Bob.

Now Aunt Peg and I were on our own, which was just the way we liked it.

"Ten acres is a lot of land to search," I said. My house was on a two-acre lot and I thought that was spacious. "Especially since these woods are so dense we can't see very far ahead of us. The shack Sean told me about could be anywhere."

"Which is why we're going to let someone who knows where it is lend us a hand. Or a paw, as the case may be."

She unzipped her parka, lifted Snowball out of his snug shelter, and set him gently down on the ground. The Maltese celebrated his freedom by giving a mighty shake that started at his head and ended at the tip of his matted tail. That done, he walked over to the nearest bush and lifted his leg. Then he sniffed the yellow snow and peed again.

"*That's* our guide?" I said with a smirk.

"Give him a minute. He's just getting his bearings. After the night he's had, I'd be very surprised if Snowball doesn't want to return to familiar surroundings. The only home he knows out here is the shack he and Pete have been living in."

Of course Aunt Peg was right. Two minutes later, Snowball was scampering along the top of the crusted snow, moving with a sense of purpose as though he had a specific goal in mind.

Aunt Peg and I slogged along behind him. In the deep woods, some of the drifts were higher than my boots. Dealing with the footing and dodging between tightly packed trees, we struggled to keep the little dog in sight.

Thank goodness for Snowball's unerring sense of direction. Even when he stopped and began to bark, it still took me a moment to pick out the cabin from the low-hanging branches that surrounded it. On my own, I might have walked right by without stopping.

As shelters went, it wasn't much. The shack was barely more than a lean-to with slatted wood sides and a tar-paper roof. I didn't see a single window and the entire structure couldn't have been more than eight feet long. It was hard to imagine that someone had actually been living there in this weather. And that he had chosen to do so. Despite its lack out outward appeal, presumably the shack was snug enough to keep its occupants warm and dry.

Aunt Peg leaned down and scooped Snowball up in her arms. "Poor pup. He probably thinks Pete is waiting for him inside."

"Have you thought about what you're going to do with him?" I asked.

Aunt Peg cast me a glance. "What's to think about?"

That was pretty much what I'd figured.

The door consisted of a single sheet of plywood. Instead of a knob, a simple latch held it closed. Aunt Peg reached for the latch, then withdrew her gloved hand. Snowball whimpered under his breath.

"This feels like an invasion of privacy," she said.

"Unfortunately for Pete, he no longer cares."

"It's still his cabin."

"Technically, it's not." I reached around her and opened the door. "Frank bought the property in its entirety. As is. So we have just as much right to be here as anyone."

The interior of the cabin looked scarcely better than the outside. There was no furniture to be seen. The cramped space held only a tiny woodstove that looked as though it served as both a source of heat and a cooktop, a sleeping bag with a moth-eaten blanket on top of it, some canned goods stacked in a corner, and a pile of assorted junk that was probably the remainder of Pete's worldly goods. It was every bit as cold inside the shack as it was without.

"Now I'm even sadder than I was before," I said.

Aunt Peg, who'd already moved through the doorway, offered not a shred of sympathy. "Buck up, Melanie. We've got work to do."

She started by sifting through the cans until she found one that held dog food. Snowball followed her every movement as she opened it up, found a bowl, and dumped it in. When she placed the bowl on the floor, the Maltese dug in eagerly.

"I suspect he's missed a meal or two," she said. "That should hold him for now. What else is there to see?"

Between us, we dug gingerly through the pile of stuff. Two shirts lay on top. Next we came to a coil of rope and a piece of tarp. Under that was a stack of old newspapers, several paperback books with broken spines, and a baggie filled with rubber bands. When we went to lift the tattered blanket beneath those finds, there was a thump, followed by a clinking noise, and then several empty bottles rolled across the floor.

Aunt Peg prodded one with her foot. "Gin. Probably Pete's last meal."

"I wonder why he went to the trouble of hiding the bottles," I said.

"If I was a psychologist I might posit that he was attempting to hide the evidence of his addiction."

"From who? Snowball?"

Mention of his name made us both look to see how the Maltese was doing. The little dog had finished his meal and disappeared.

"There." I pointed toward the other end of the room. "He's burrowed inside the sleeping bag."

Aunt Peg sighed. "That poor dog knows something is very wrong. He just can't figure out what he needs to do to fix it." She leaned down and slipped her hand into the bedding. "Come out here, you little scamp."

The lump at the foot of the bedroll didn't move. Abruptly, Aunt Peg frowned and withdrew her hand. Her fingers were clenched around a small, rectangular object.

"What do you suppose this is?" she asked.

We walked to the doorway and examined it in the light.

"It looks like an old wooden matchbox."

"Indeed. I think you're right." Aunt Peg gave the box a small shake. "And there's something inside."

She used her thumb to slide the inner compartment open. We both leaned in for a closer look. The box held just two things: a tiny tooth and a ring.

"That's a puppy canine," Aunt Peg said. "Probably one of Snowball's."

I was more interested in the ring. I reached inside with my fingertips and fished it out. The bauble felt heavy in my hand. It was thick and made of silver, with a flat, deep-set reddish stone and engraving around the crown.

"This looks like a high school ring." I examined the initials that circled the gemstone. "What school is SCHS?"

"I haven't the slightest idea," said Aunt Peg. "But I suppose we should take it along and give it to the police. If they locate Pete's family, his relatives might want the ring back."

"I'm not sure the police will even bother to look for Pete's family," I said. "They didn't sound particularly interested."

As I slipped the ring in my pocket, Snowball emerged from the sleeping bag. When he saw us standing in the doorway, his tail began to wag. He scampered across the floor to join us. Even filthy and matted, the Maltese was pretty cute. He certainly deserved better than this.

"That's not the only thing Pete's family might want back," I pointed out.

Aunt Peg frowned. "I'll cross that bridge when I come to it."

Chapter
Six

Monday morning I went to school.

After the four-day Thanksgiving holiday, I was dragging a bit when I entered the hallowed halls of Howard Academy, where I worked as a special needs tutor. The school was situated high on a hilltop near downtown Greenwich. I'd always thought its location was fitting, considering that the private academy's lofty objective was the guidance, development, and education of America's future leaders.

Years earlier, when I was new to Howard Academy, that mission statement had sounded boastful to me. I quickly discovered I was wrong. HA numbered congressmen, ambassadors, and a vice president among its illustrious alumni. Not to mention too many titans of industry to count.

A heritage like that was enough to keep all of us

teachers on our toes. If we were ever tempted to let standards slip—even for a moment—Headmaster Russell Hanover II was always on hand to ensure that everything remained up to snuff. His words, not mine.

Mr. Hanover was a strict disciplinarian and a stickler for school rules, but he allowed me to bring Faith to work with me. For that, I would forgive the man just about anything. My Poodle held court on a cedar-filled bed in the corner of my classroom, and the students who arrived for tutoring greeted Faith with a great deal more enthusiasm than they ever lavished upon me.

I wasn't complaining about that. Whatever brought kids through my door with a smile on their faces was fine by me.

The current semester's schedule left my afternoons free on Tuesdays and Thursdays. Bowing to parental pressure, Howard Academy also offered early dismissal on Fridays—a perk that enabled students' families to get a jump on their weekend getaways to Aspen, Wellington, or Fishers Island.

I wasn't aware that Frank was privy to the details of my calendar, but Bertie must have clued him in because Faith and I had barely left the school on Tuesday afternoon when my phone rang. I grimaced when I glanced at the screen. Faith, who was riding shotgun, looked at me and wrinkled her nose. She was clearly counseling me not to pick up.

"It's Frank," I told her. "If I don't talk to him now, he'll just call back."

Faith just sighed. That was easy to understand. I felt much the same way.

"Hey Mel," Frank said cheerfully when I'd put the phone to my ear. "I have a job for you."

"Thanks, but no thanks. I already have a job."

"Yeah, but this one's fun."

Somehow I doubted that. If it was fun, Frank would already be doing it and he wouldn't need me.

"Think about it," he said. "Davey's bus doesn't bring him home until later and Sam's got Kevin until you get back. So you've got a couple free hours that you could spend up here in Wilton. Bob and I are working overtime to get Haney's Holiday Home ready to open for business this weekend. We could really use an extra pair of hands."

"What about Claire?" I asked.

"She was here all morning."

"Bertie?"

"New baby. She already has her hands full."

Now I was getting desperate. "Aunt Peg?"

There was a long pause. Then Frank said, "You're kidding, right?"

Yes, I supposed I was.

"Where's your family spirit?" asked Frank.

Right about then it occurred to me that it would probably take less time to help my brother than it would to win the argument. Half an hour later, Faith and I were approaching the tree farm's driveway. In the forty-eight hours since my previous visit, there had already been at least one improvement. Someone had repainted and rehung the sign. I decided to take that as a good omen.

Faith loved to visit new places. She was standing on her seat, wagging her tail, when I parked next to Frank's Jeep. As soon as I opened the car door, the big Poodle hopped out and began to explore. We were at least a quarter mile from the road, so I let her run around for a few minutes before we went inside.

Like the sign at the end of the driveway, the office building had already seen some repairs. The rotting step had been replaced and the banister beside it now felt solid beneath my hand. The porch was neatly swept and the windows on either side of the door glistened from a recent cleaning. The doorknob turned easily and the door itself swung inward without complaint.

Best of all, the electricity had been turned on and the woodstove was lit. The room that Faith and I entered was bright and wonderfully warm. I had to give Frank credit. This was an amazing, inviting change from the dark, gloomy space I'd visited just two days earlier.

Speaking of Frank, he had drop cloths spread across the floor and a long-handled paint roller in his hands. Half the back wall was still a dingy shade of gray, but the remainder was already sporting a coat of cheerful yellow paint. Frank set down the roller as I closed the door behind us. He turned and greeted us with a grin.

"So," he said, spreading his hands wide. "What do you think?"

"I'm impressed."

My brother peered at me intently. "Does that mean you're impressed like, *Considering it's Frank, he didn't screw up too badly,* or as in you really like what you see?"

"Definitely the latter." I thought about what he'd said, then added, "Am I really that hard on you?"

Frank didn't even hesitate. "Yes."

"Still?"

"I guess you're improving a little," Frank admitted. "Maybe you're mellowing with age."

Not a comforting thought.

"Where's Bob?" I asked. "I thought he'd be here helping too."

"He left a little while ago to go iron out the details on the business license and tax ID number. Then he's going to stop by The Bean Counter and make sure everything's running smoothly there."

Frank crossed the room, crouched down, and greeted Faith with a thumping pat on the head. She preferred a caress with more finesse, but subtlety wasn't Frank's strong suit. Nor has he ever understood my passion for Poodles. As far as Frank was concerned, all my big black dogs were interchangeable. But at least he'd made the effort to acknowledge her presence.

Faith was no dummy. She redirected Frank's energy by sitting down and offering him a paw to shake. Surprised, my brother rocked back on his heels and sputtered a laugh.

"Did you see that?"

"Of course," I told him. "Faith is saying hello to you."

Frank shook her paw gently, then rose to his feet. "I have two kids now, you know."

"Of course I know that." I took off my coat and hung it on a hook by the door. "Bertie's been so busy that I've barely seen her since Josh was born. I am well aware of the addition to your family."

"Aunt Peg thinks that children should grow up with a puppy."

No surprise there.

"Aunt Peg thinks that *everyone* should have a puppy," I said.

"We didn't when we were little," Frank pointed out.

"I guess we weren't as lucky as some kids."

His head dipped in a brief nod. "Anyway, I just wanted you to know I'm thinking about it."

"Good for you." If I pushed, Frank would push back. So instead I changed the subject. "I'm here and I'm all yours for the next two hours. What do you want me to do?"

"There's a can of white paint and some smaller brushes behind the counter. How are you with trim? A fresh coat of paint on the window frames would really brighten things up."

Faith lay down on the floor near the stove while Frank and I worked in companionable silence for the next hour and a half. Between applying coats of paint, I sifted through the collection of holiday decorations—delivered that morning by Claire—that were spread across the countertop.

There were giant tinsel garlands, gaudy ornaments, roping made of Christmas ribbons, and even an inflatable life-size Santa Claus. Claire had also managed to find several sets of holiday-themed curtains depicting the flight of Santa's sleigh. The woman was a marvel. I closed my eyes and imagined everything in place. Once the paint was dry and the decorations hung, the office would be totally transformed.

Faith lifted her head and a moment later I felt a draft of cold air as the office door opened behind me. A stocky, middle-aged man with ruddy cheeks and a bristling black moustache came walking inside. His head was entirely bald and the tips of his ears were bright pink. In this weather, I was surprised he wasn't wearing a hat.

Frank looked up. "I'm sorry, we're not open for business yet. Could you come back this weekend? We plan to be up and running by Saturday morning."

"No problem." The man held up a hand. "I don't need a tree. I'm just here looking for a friend of mine. A guy about my age, brown hair, blue eyes? His name is Pete. This is the address he gave me."

Frank and I exchanged a look.

"Who are you?" I asked.

"John Smith." The man stuck out his hand for me to shake. "And yes, that's my real name. My parents had a weird sense of humor. Pete's a bit of a wanderer and he doesn't have a phone. But he told last month that if I needed to find him, this was the place to come. He missed a meeting we were supposed to go to, so I thought I'd better come and check on him. Have you seen him?"

"I'm afraid I have some bad news for you," I said. "Pete was involved in an accident over the weekend."

"Is he okay?"

"No, he's not. I'm very sorry to have to tell you that Pete was killed."

"Killed?" John Smith shook his head. "I think you're mistaken."

I flipped the tarp off the old rocking chair and dragged it across the room. "I'm sure the news has come as a shock. Maybe you should sit down."

"Hell, no, I don't want to sit down." Smith glared at the chair, then back up at Frank and me. His gaze narrowed. "What I want is to know what happened to Pete. Are you people the Haneys?"

"No, I'm Melanie Travis," I said. "And this is my brother, Frank Turnbull. Frank and his partner are the new owners of this tree farm—"

"Since when?"

"Last week," Frank answered.

"Last week, Pete was alive," Smith said. "I just saw him. And now you're telling me he's dead?"

"Yes, I'm afraid so. There was an accident—"

"Don't tell me he was hit by a car." John Smith, who'd been so certain that he didn't need a seat, now sank down into the rocking chair anyway. It creaked beneath his weight. "Did that little dog of his run out in the road? I told him he needed a leash for that mutt. Heck, I even offered to buy him one if he'd use it."

"It wasn't a car accident," Frank said.

"Then what the hell happened?"

"It appears that Pete had had quite a bit to drink," I told him. "He was out in the woods with Snowball. A tree branch hit him on the head and knocked him unconscious. By the time he was found he had died of exposure."

Smith frowned as he listened to my explanation. At the end he said, "You're sure about that?"

Frank and I both nodded.

"And you're sure the man that was found in the woods was Pete?"

"The police identified him," I said. "They told us Pete was a homeless man who'd been hanging around town for years. Apparently they were quite familiar with him."

"And they told you he was drunk?"

Frank nodded. "The EMTs could smell the gin on him. And the police said Pete's drinking had been out of control for years."

"But not recently," Smith muttered.

"Excuse me?" I said.

"There's something wrong with your story. Things didn't happen the way you're telling me they did."

"We're not making up a story," Frank told him. "We're telling you what happened. If you don't believe us, you can talk to the police. They'll confirm what we've said."

Smith pushed himself up out of the chair. He walked over to a window and stared out into the woods for a minute before turning to face us again. "I'm not accusing you of lying. I'm just telling you that things don't add up."

"In what way?" I asked.

"The Pete you're describing is the man he used to be. Not the man I've gotten to know over these last few months. Sure, he'd had his problems with alcohol. He was the first to admit that the juice brought out the devil in him. But Pete finally realized that his addiction had cost him just about everything that mattered. That was why he decided it was time to turn his life around."

"What are you saying?" I asked.

"Pete joined a substance abuse program in August. That's how we met. I've seen men who join up because they feel obliged to go through the motions. But that wasn't Pete. He was motivated. He really wanted to change. That was why I became his sponsor. And I'm telling you flat out that's why your story doesn't make sense. Pete hadn't had a drop to drink in more than three months."

Chapter
Seven

"That can't be right." Suddenly it felt as though the room was tilting. I thought I might need that chair myself.

"Trust me. I know what I'm talking about. Last time I saw Pete was four days ago."

"That would have been Saturday," I said.

"The day he died," Frank added.

John Smith nodded. "Saturday afternoon Pete was sharp, sober, and in an optimistic frame of mind about the direction his life was heading. And now you're telling me that a few hours later he was falling-down drunk? Nope. It didn't happen."

"Maybe you didn't know Pete as well as you thought you did," I ventured.

"I'm betting I knew him better than you did."

That wasn't saying much.

"My aunt and I had a look around Pete's cabin after he died," I told him. "We were hoping to find something that would tell us who he was and where he'd come from."

"And did you?"

I shook my head. "But what we did find was a cache of empty alcohol bottles hidden under a blanket."

"Empty," Smith said. "You found *empty* bottles."

"Which means that somebody had drunk their contents," Frank said.

"Somebody." Smith strode across the room toward the door. "But not Pete."

He reached for the knob. Before he could leave, I asked, "What was Pete's last name?"

That made him pause. "I don't know," he admitted. "It's not required. He never told us."

"Where was he from?"

"Pete wasn't big on sharing information of a personal nature with the group. That was his prerogative. We were there to support him in his journey, not to grill him about his past."

"It sounds like maybe you didn't know Pete very well, either," Frank said.

John Smith let himself out and slammed the door behind him.

On the way home from the Christmas tree farm, I stopped at Aunt Peg's house. Yes, strictly speaking,

Greenwich isn't located between Wilton and Stamford. But if ever there was a good time for a necessary detour, this seemed like the one.

Aunt Peg and her pack of Standard Poodles—all of whom were related in various ways to the Poodles at my house—were universally delighted to see us. While Faith and that canine crew raced around the fenced backyard renewing their acquaintance, Aunt Peg and I went inside. She led the way to her kitchen.

Together we stepped over the baby gate across the doorway. That was new. Then I realized why it was there. Snowball was lying in a plush dog bed beside the butcher-block table. The little dog jumped up and ran over to greet us.

I reached down and gave him a gentle pat. "If I hadn't known who this was, I wouldn't have recognized him."

The Maltese's formerly tangled and dirty coat was now white, silky, and mat-free. Aunt Peg had also trimmed him, shaping the hair so that it framed Snowball's body. A small barrette on the top of his head held up the topknot hair that had previously fallen forward over his eyes.

"It's amazing what you can accomplish with a good bath and a pair of scissors. Snowball managed it all beautifully. He's very well socialized for a dog who has probably led a mostly solitary life. But there are notable gaps in his training—housebreaking being chief among them. He's confined to one room until we have that figured out, but as you can see, he has adapted to life here quite happily."

"He looks great," I said. The Maltese snatched up a furry toy mouse and began to bounce around the floor, squeaking the toy with each joyful leap. "Has anyone from Wilton called to check on him?"

"I haven't heard a single peep from the police or animal control, which is all to the good. It would be a shame if the authorities decided they wanted to take custody and he had to be uprooted again so quickly. They seem to have forgotten about him and that suits me just fine."

Aunt Peg pulled out a chair at the table and took a seat. "Since you're here, I'm sure you must have something interesting to tell me. Sit down and spit it out."

It didn't take long to relate the conversation Frank and I had had earlier with Pete's sponsor.

"John Smith," she said when I was finished. "What kind of name is that?"

"Plain. Basic?"

"Maybe it's an alias," Aunt Peg mused. She takes great delight in suspecting everyone of everything.

"Only an idiot would choose an alias like John Smith," I pointed out.

Instead of replying, Aunt Peg got up and left the room. While I was awaiting her return, I made myself a cup of coffee. Instant. The only kind Aunt Peg keeps on hand for visitors who won't join her in sipping Earl Grey tea.

"The results of Pete's autopsy aren't available yet," she announced upon her return.

"How do you know that?"

"I called the Wilton medical examiner's office and told them I was a concerned citizen checking up on a recent death."

"And that *worked*?"

"I got the answer, didn't I? Now tell me what else Mr. Smith said."

"I've already told you everything. He said he'd last seen Pete Saturday afternoon, and that there was no way Pete got drunk that night."

"Despite the empty bottles we found?"

"Despite everything apparently. John Smith was quite adamant about what he knew."

"With a name like John Smith, I suppose you'd have to be an adamant sort," Aunt Peg decided. "Otherwise you'd get lost in the crowd."

"What if the gin the EMTs smelled was on Pete's clothing?" I'd been thinking about that on the way there. I paused to let her consider the possibility, then said, "Somebody might have spilled it on him. Maybe on purpose."

"Somebody like who?"

That was the $64,000 question. If indeed it was a question we should be asking at all.

"Pete was homeless," I said. "He had few belongings and not even a fixed address. Who would want to harm a man who had nothing?"

"I have no idea," Aunt Peg replied. "But I'm beginning to think that it might not be a bad idea to find out. An accidental death on a piece of property recently acquired by the family is a misfortune. A murder on that same land has the makings of a catastrophe."

"Pete froze to death in the snow," I pointed out.

"*After* being bonked on the head—by a conveniently falling tree branch, no less." Aunt Peg frowned. "Why did we ever believe that was an accident?"

"Because the police told us it was?"

"Oh pish. The police don't even know who Pete was or where he came from. Why should we believe everything they say?"

Her eyes lit up with a familiar fervor and I knew what she was thinking. *Especially when the alternative was so intriguing*.

"We don't know anything about Pete either," I said.

"Then clearly we should attempt to remedy that. It seems to me that the only clue we possess is the ring we found in Pete's cabin. What did you do with it?"

"I have it here. I put it in my purse for safekeeping."

"Let's have another look and see what it tells us."

I produced the chunky ring and handed it over. Aunt Peg nestled it briefly in her palm. "SCHS. I would think those are the school's initials. With luck, it will be somewhere in Connecticut. At any rate, that's where I'll begin my search. We'll see what we can discover, shall we?"

There was a laptop sitting on the counter. Aunt Peg brought it over to the table. While she went to work, I reached down and lifted Snowball into my lap. Each of our Standard Poodles weighed more than fifty pounds. And Bud was close to twenty. Though I was accustomed to having dogs in my lap, I wasn't used to handling one who could be cupped between my two hands.

Snowball stood up on my legs, braced his front feet against my chest, and gave my sweater a very thorough sniff. No doubt he was checking out the scents my dogs had left there. When I returned home, I was sure the Poodles would subject me to the same treatment.

On the other side of the table, Aunt Peg was hunched over and frowning at the computer screen. Loathe to break her concentration, I reached around Snowball and picked up the ring. I held it between my thumb and forefinger and lifted it up to the light.

Immediately I saw something neither Aunt Peg nor

I had noticed earlier. There was writing on the inside of the band. I lowered the ring and squinted at the tiny print. One side was engraved with a set of initials: PCD. The other had a date, presumably the year of graduation: 1994.

"I've found something," I said.

Aunt Peg looked up. "So have I. There's a good chance that the initials on that ring stand for Stonebridge Central High School."

Stonebridge was a small town located on the Connecticut coast between Fairfield and Bridgeport. I'd seen the Stonebridge exit on the Connecticut Turnpike, but I'd never had a reason to go there. I suspected that was about to change.

I passed the ring back to Aunt Peg. "Look inside."

She did, then smiled with satisfaction. "How did we miss this the first time around?"

"Because we weren't looking. I was planning to give the ring to the police, remember?"

"Well, it's a good thing you didn't. Obviously the *P* is for Peter. The *C*, maybe Charles? *D* . . . *d* . . . *d* . . ." She drummed her fingers on the tabletop. "Dalton? Dreyer? Dunleavy?"

"I bet somebody at Stonebridge Central High School can tell me what those initials stand for. Or if not, I'd imagine they'll let me have a look at their 1994 yearbook. I'll pay the school a visit on Thursday afternoon."

"That's two full days from now!"

I looked at her askance. "What's your point?"

"I should think you'd be more eager to uncover Pete's backstory."

"Yes, but I'm also eager to keep my job. I have classes all day tomorrow at Howard Academy."

"I suppose that's a decent excuse," Aunt Peg grumbled.

Indeed.

Thursday morning, I told Sam that I'd be making a side trip to Stonebridge after school.

My husband was standing at the stove, scrambling eggs. I was checking to make sure that all of Davey's homework was inside his backpack, and looking for Kevin's missing sneaker. Since both the shoe and Bud had disappeared at approximately the same time, I was pretty sure I knew where to start my search.

"What's in Stonebridge?" Sam asked over his shoulder.

"A high school with the same initials as the ones on Pete's ring. It's possible he was a former student there, and I'm hoping I can get information about him."

I had told Sam what John Smith had said during his visit to the tree farm. I'd also mentioned that Aunt Peg and I were troubled by this new information. Then I'd left the rest to Sam's imagination. We've been around this block before. He had to know what would happen next.

Now he simply turned back to the stove and said, "Stonebridge isn't far. I assume you'll be home in time for dinner?"

"Of course."

"Because if not, I can take the boys out for pizza."

"Pizza?" Kevin looked up with interest.

"Not now," I told him. "Later."

"Found it." Davey entered the kitchen, holding Kevin's sneaker. Predictably, Bud was nowhere to be seen. "It needs a new lace."

"I have spares. Where's your math homework?"

Davey handed me a shoe that was wet with slime, but otherwise mostly intact. "I finished it at school yesterday. History was boring. I needed something to do."

"History isn't boring," Sam told him. "It's the foundation upon which civilization is built."

"Says the man with a degree in computer science." I sniffed the air delicately. "Are those eggs burning?"

"No." He leaned in for a closer look. "They could be a little well-done. Who's ready for eggs?"

"Me!" cried Kev.

He jumped in the air and knocked over a wooden bowl that was filled with unshelled walnuts. The bowl went careening off the counter and the nuts hit the hard wood floor with a splatter that sounded like gunfire. Dogs came running from all directions.

Davey and I both dove to the floor. We scooped up nuts as fast as we could. Kevin squealed with laughter. Sam dished out the eggs.

Mealtime is an adventure around here.

Chapter
Eight

I hated taking a Poodle somewhere with me, then making her wait in the car. Especially Faith. But that afternoon she was out of luck, because when I left Howard Academy, I drove straight up the turnpike to Stonebridge.

GPS directed me to the town's high school and we arrived while classes were still in session. Even though it was December, I chose my parking space with care to ensure that the temperature inside the car would remain comfortable while I was gone.

Then I had to explain to Faith that not all schools were as understanding as Howard Academy about big black dogs roaming through their hallways. She sat and listened in stoic silence. When I locked the car, Faith was lying across the backseat with her head nestled sadly between her front paws. That Poodle knew a dozen different ways to make me feel guilty and she wasn't above exploiting every single one of them.

Stonebridge Central High looked like any number of other public schools I'd seen. The single-story building was long and rectangular. Constructed primarily of brick and concrete, its stern façade was softened only by a long row of classroom windows. A sidewalk that wrapped around the parking lot led me to the portico-covered front door.

I walked through the door into a large lobby. Wide hallways on either side led to classrooms. Directly across from the entrance was a well-lit display case whose shelves were filled with sports trophies, team pictures, and a big red banner reading GO ROCKIES!

Rockies? Stonebridge? I supposed that was cute.

Next to the display case was a door marked OFFICE. Easy peasy. I knocked once, then opened the door and let myself in. A woman seated behind a metal desk popped her head sideways around a computer screen.

"Can I help you?"

I introduced myself and explained that I was seeking information about a possible former student.

"Mrs. LaRue is our assistant principal. She might be able to help you. Let me see if she's busy." The woman got up and went into a side room whose door was sitting partially open.

While a murmured conversation took place in the other office, I surveyed my surroundings. I was pleased to see a long shelf holding a row of SCHS yearbooks that appeared to date back through several decades. If Mrs. LaRue wasn't able to help me, hopefully I could get permission to peruse the yearbooks for clues.

After a minute, both women emerged from the inner office. Sharon LaRue walked straight over to me. We introduced ourselves and sized each other up.

Sharon was a solid woman in her early forties who looked like a former college athlete. She had broad shoulders, a direct gaze, and a grip that was strong enough to make my fingers tingle. Her brown hair was pulled back in a tight ponytail and she had a cardigan sweater draped across her shoulders.

"Carol tells me you're trying to locate one of our former students?" she said.

"Yes. If you have a few minutes free, I'd love to ask you about him."

Sharon nodded, ushered me deftly into her office, and shut the door behind us. Her manner was both stern and approachable, a combination of traits that must have been useful in her current position. She waved me into a seat and walked around behind her desk.

"What's the student's name?" she asked.

"That's part of the problem. I don't know. In fact, I'm not even sure he *was* a student here. His first name was Pete and this ring was found among his belongings." I withdrew the piece of jewelry from my pocket and handed it over. "I'm hoping it's a 1994 class ring from your school. The initials *PCD* are engraved on the inside."

Sharon glanced down at the ring, then back at me. She closed her hand, wrapping her fingers firmly around the heavy bauble.

Something in her expression prompted me to say, "You know who he is, don't you?"

"I might," she allowed. "But before we go any further, I need you to explain why you're interested in this information."

"My brother recently purchased a piece of property in Wilton. After the fact, he discovered that Pete was a squatter who sometimes made use of a cabin there. Last Sunday morning, Pete's body was found on the property. He'd frozen to death in the snow."

Blood drained from the woman's face. She clutched either side of the desk for support, then slowly sank into her seat. "Dead?" she choked out the word. "Pete is *dead*?"

"Yes." I nodded slowly. "I'm sorry to have broken the news to you so bluntly. I'm assuming you knew him?"

"Oh yes, I knew Pete." Sharon's expression was bleak. "Years ago, I knew him quite well. He and I were high school sweethearts, right here at Central High. As soon as you handed me the ring, I knew it had to be his. Peter Charles Dempsey. We grew up together in Stonebridge. His family still lives here."

She opened her hand and extended it toward me. I took back the ring.

"You're sure it's his?"

"Yes, there's no doubt. This isn't a huge school. I'm quite certain it was the only ring with those initials made that year."

"How long had it been since you'd seen Pete?" I asked.

Sharon thought back. "It must be at least five years since he left town. Nobody seemed to know where he went."

I sat back in my seat. "Why did he leave?"

"For several years before that Pete had been having . . . problems."

"What kind of problems?"

Sharon didn't answer.

"Professional problems?" I prodded. "Personal?"

After a few seconds, she gave a small shrug. "I suppose under the circumstances, it doesn't matter if I talk to you. Especially since everything I have to say is already common knowledge around town. Stonebridge isn't a large community. There are families who have been here for generations. At times it seems like everybody knows everyone else's business."

"Where did Pete fit in?" I said.

"The Dempseys are one of the older families in town. Pete's parents and grandparents were successful and well-connected. He was raised with the expectation that he would succeed at any endeavor he put his hand to. In high school, Pete played football, he was on the debate team, he got good grades. It seemed like he could do no wrong."

Her eyes became misty. I wondered if she was remembering her former beau the way he'd been. I gave her a minute, then said gently, "What happened?"

"He grew up. I guess we all did. Even those of us who went away to college, came back." Sharon glanced around her cozy office. "Stonebridge is just that kind of place."

I nodded encouragingly.

"Pete married Penelope and they started a family. He and two of his friends, Larry Potts and Owen Strunk, started an executive search firm. There's plenty of business to be had in Fairfield County and it took off right away. The three of them were flying high."

"That all sounds great," I said. "So what changed?"

"Bit by bit, things began to fall apart. Pete's father passed away and his mother went into a deep depression. Then Pete began quarreling with his business partners. I suspect the dissatisfaction at work affected his home life too. Pete had always enjoyed tossing back a few beers, but over time it became more that that. He'd start drinking and then it was as though he didn't know how to stop."

"Pete became an alcoholic," I said.

"I guess that's what you would call it," Sharon

agreed reluctantly. "All I know is that the man he became had little in common with the boy I'd thought I'd known."

"Life changes everyone," I said. "Some people learn to roll with the punches. Others fall down."

"Pete didn't fall down, he just . . . disappeared. One day he was here and the next he was gone."

"Didn't anyone look for him?" I asked curiously.

"Oh sure. I'd imagine Larry and Owen must have. Although by that time I wouldn't be surprised if they were relieved not to have to deal with him anymore."

"What about his wife, Penelope?"

"Ex-wife," Sharon corrected me. "He left shortly after their divorce became final. Penelope said he'd told her he needed a change of scenery."

"What about his friends?" I asked. "Any other family?"

Sharon just shrugged. "It's not like I was keeping tabs. Pete and I were over a long time ago. What he did and where he went wasn't any of my business anymore."

And yet, I thought, she seemed remarkably well-informed about Pete's adult life. Perhaps that was a function of living in such a close-knit community.

"Are you saying you don't care that he ended up as a vagrant, living on the streets in Wilton?"

Sharon frowned. "I'm sorry Pete's dead. He deserved a better end than that. But it's not as though he and I were still close."

"Is Pete's mother still alive?" I asked.

"Yes, although I gather Betty Dempsey is not well. Pete's younger brother, Tyler, has moved back home to take care of her." She stopped and swallowed heavily as a sudden thought struck her. "They must not have heard the news. Otherwise everyone would be talking about it."

"The police might not have been able to identify Pete yet," I said. "On Sunday, all they had to go on was his first name. No one knew who Pete was until you recognized his ring a few minutes ago."

Sharon stared at me across the desk. "Tyler needs to be told about what happened to his brother. You have to go see him and do that. Then he can break the news to his mother."

I was already shaking my head. "The Wilton police—"

"The Wilton police aren't here. *You are.* Nobody asked you to come to Stonebridge but you did. I answered your questions; now you need to do your part. Betty and Tyler are Pete's family. They deserve to hear the news from someone who was there."

Sharon opened a computer that was sitting on the side of her desk. She typed something, waited a minute, then turned the screen in my direction. "Is this the man you found?"

I'd only glanced at Pete's body for a moment before quickly looking away. Even so, I hadn't been able to forget what I'd seen. An image of Pete's face had stayed with me. Now I saw that same face staring out at me from the computer. The man in the picture on the screen was younger, sleeker, healthier looking. But the two were undeniably one and the same.

Sharon didn't wait for me to answer. Instead, she snapped the computer shut and said, "That's what I thought. The Dempseys are at one-eighty-three Meadow Lane. It's just outside of town. I'll call Tyler and tell him to expect you."

Faith was delighted by my return and not at all amused when I drove three miles, then left her behind in the car once again.

The Dempseys lived on a quiet residential street that was lined with mature trees. Their branches, now bare, met to form a canopy across the middle of the road. In another season, the effect must have been shady and welcoming. But now, the tangle of intertwined tree limbs snaking upward toward the stark winter sky made me shiver and wish that I'd tied my scarf more tightly around my neck.

"Don't worry," I told Faith. "This time I won't be gone long."

The Dempsey home was an older colonial with white siding and freshly painted black shutters. A brick walkway led me to the front stairs. As I approached, the door opened. Sharon must have kept her word and called ahead.

The man standing in the doorway—Tyler Dempsey, I assumed—didn't look pleased to see me. The pinched expression on his face was accentuated by his thin lips and high forehead. Tyler had a slender build and the cashmere pullover he was wearing did nothing to add bulk to his narrow chest. His long, pale fingers rested on the doorknob as if he wanted to be prepared to slam the door shut at a moment's notice.

That wasn't reassuring.

He waited until I'd climbed the three steps and was standing right in front of him before speaking, "You must be Melanie Travis. Sharon LaRue warned me about you."

"Excuse me?" I tipped back my head to look up at him. "She was the one who wanted me to come here. Are you Tyler Dempsey?"

"I am."

"I'm afraid I need to talk to you about your brother." I looked past him into the empty foyer. "Maybe we could step inside for a minute?"

"I don't think that will be necessary. Nothing you could say about Pete would surprise me. What did my brother do now?"

"Are you sure you want to have this conversation outside?" This wasn't at all how I'd pictured delivering the news of Pete's demise.

"Quite sure. Did Pete send you—is that why you're here? What does he need this time? Money? A place to stay? Someone to bail him out of jail? I'm sorry, Ms. Travis, but whatever convincing sob story my brother told you to bring you to my door, I assure we've heard it all before."

They hadn't heard *this* before, I thought meanly. Apparently my only option was to deliver the news standing on his steps.

"Pete Dempsey is dead," I said. "He died of exposure last Saturday night in Wilton."

"Dead?" Tyler cocked an eyebrow disdainfully. Other than that, his face betrayed no emotion. You might have thought I'd told him that the chef at his club was out of caviar.

"I'm sorry to be the bearer of bad news," I added.

"Yes, that is bad news," Tyler agreed in a flat tone. "Where did the unfortunate event take place?"

"At a Christmas tree farm, Haney's Holiday Home, in Wilton."

"What was my brother doing at a Christmas tree farm?"

"There was a cabin in the woods. A small shack, really. He appeared to be living there."

"Well." Tyler frowned. "That part sounds about right."

"The Wilton police can give you more details about your brother's death," I told him. "I'm sure they'll be relieved to hear from his next of kin."

"I'll take care of that. And see what arrangements need to be made."

Once again I gazed into the house. "Perhaps I could offer my condolences to your mother?"

"No, that won't be possible. Mother isn't well. News like this would be upsetting to her and, in her condition, that wouldn't be good at all."

I should hope she'd find the news upsetting, I thought. But frankly, Tyler didn't look terribly undone by the revelation of his brother's death. Pete's descent into alcoholism must have been painful for his family. And perhaps humiliating. Even so, I wasn't sure that excused the lack of emotion with which Tyler had absorbed the news.

"Thank you for doing your duty," he said shortly. "Now you should be on your way."

Tyler stepped back and shut the door between us.

"Wait!" Belatedly I remembered I'd brought something to give to him. "I have your brother's school ring."

The door didn't budge. I heard the lock click into place.

If there had been a mail slot, I might have pushed the ring through. Instead, I shoved it back in my pocket.

It seemed odd that Tyler had never asked for any details about what had happened. He hadn't even appeared to be curious. The police had dismissed Pete's death as an alcohol-related accident. His friend, John Smith, was sure Pete hadn't had a drop to drink in months. Whichever version was the truth, Pete's only sibling hadn't even wanted to hear about it.

Even after I'd made it clear that Pete no longer wanted anything from him, Tyler had been chiefly concerned with getting rid of me. I wondered what I should make of that.

Chapter
Nine

When I turned and started down the steps, I saw a tiny woman standing on the sidewalk next to the Volvo. She was bundled up against the cold in a long, puffy coat with a hood trimmed in fake fur. There were thick-soled boots on her feet and her hand, extended toward the car, was encased in a bright red mitten.

Faith was wise in the ways of the world. She knew better than to throw herself against the car window, barking at someone she couldn't reach. Instead, she was sitting upright on the seat, looking at the woman quizzically through the glass. As I drew near, I realized that the two of them appeared to be holding a conversation.

"Her name is Faith," I said when I reached the sidewalk.

The woman turned. Clear blue eyes peered up at me from a face that was wrinkled and covered in age spots. Several wisps of gray hair escaped from beneath the hood and fluttered in the breeze.

She smiled and said, "I'm Stella. Stella Braverman. That's a pretty dog in there. Is she a Poodle?"

"Yes. She's a Standard."

"I used to have a couple of Poodles, Chloe and Pierre. They weren't that big, though. I think they were Mini size. They were great dogs. I wish I could have another but at my age, I don't want to get a pet I might not outlive. Because then what would happen to it when I was gone?"

"Maybe your family—?"

"No, there's just me. Even my friends are dying off now. Old age isn't for weenies. Don't let anyone ever tell you differently. What's your name? I don't think you said."

"Melanie Travis," I told her.

"I saw you were visiting the Dempseys. Are you a friend of Betty's?"

"No, although I was hoping to speak with her for a few minutes."

"And Tyler left you standing on the step." Stella shook her head. "That boy needs to learn some manners. Although in his case, it's probably too late. I've known Betty since before he was born, and some days he tries to keep me away too. Tells me she's feeling too poorly to see me."

"Is she very ill?" I asked.

"Cancer." Stella whispered the word as though it was too awful to say out loud. "Betty doesn't have more than a few months left. Leastwise, that's what the doctors tell her. So if Tyler thinks I'm not going to visit my best friend now, he can think again. I've had a key to the back door of that house for fifty years, same as Betty has one for my house. As soon as Tyler goes off somewhere in his car, I'm in there like a shot."

She looked up and winked. "Kids. They don't know as much as they think they do. So what did you want to see Betty about?"

"I'm afraid it's complicated," I said.

"Good. I like complicated. Let's go inside and get warm and you can tell me all about it. Bring Faith along too. She doesn't look very happy sitting in that car all by herself. Do you like herb tea? If not, you should drink it anyway because it's good for you. How about Fig Newtons? I just got a new box yesterday at the supermarket."

There was something surprisingly comforting about placing myself in Stella's hands and simply following her directions. Plus, she struck me as the kind of woman who wouldn't take no for an answer.

Five minutes later, Faith and I were seated in her front parlor. Stella came in from the kitchen carrying a small tray that held two delicate china cups and a plate of cookies. Now that she'd shed her bulky outerwear, the elderly woman looked even smaller than she had outside. I jumped up to take the tray from her, but Stella waved me away and set it down on the coffee table between two love seats.

"I found a couple of shortbread cookies in the pantry for Faith," she said. "They're pretty stale, but she probably won't mind. I read online that you're not supposed to feed dogs raisins. Did you know that?"

"Yes. No grapes or chocolate either."

"Well, then I guess you're on top of things. Raisins and figs seem kind of similar to me. So I figured better safe than sorry."

Stella handed Faith a shortbread cookie. The Poodle swept it gently out of her hand. Stella watched with satisfaction as Faith chewed and swallowed the cookie. Then she sat down on the other love seat.

She handed me a flower-sprigged cup and saucer, and picked up the other set for herself. "Now then, suppose you tell me what's complicated?"

I started with my brother's purchase of Mr. Haney's Christmas tree farm. I didn't know exactly why, except that Stella seemed like she would enjoy a good story. I wasn't surprised that she made a great audience.

Stella concentrated as she listened. Her attention was focused on me like a laser. When I got to the part about finding Pete's body in the snow, she issued an audible gasp.

"I'm sorry," I said with a guilty wince. I'd gotten so caught up in telling the tale that I hadn't thought to soften the news. "You must have known Pete too. I shouldn't have just blurted that out."

"You don't need to apologize on my account. It's poor Betty I'm worried about." Stella sighed. "This will come as a real blow to her. The rest of us . . . well, it's been five years. I guess we all suspected that something had gone terribly wrong. But Betty still held out hope that she would see Pete one more time in this life. When she got the diagnosis, she even sent Tyler out looking for him, hoping he could track him down. But nothing ever came of his efforts."

"I'm very sorry," I said again. The words felt wholly inadequate.

"For pity's sake, don't keep apologizing." Stella waved me off again. Apparently she was good at that. She dropped her hand beneath the table and slipped Faith another cookie. She was good at that too. "To tell the truth, in some ways it was a relief when Pete went away. Of course, at the time nobody suspected that he wouldn't come back. But let's just say that most of us were ready for a break. That boy's life was one big drama."

I finally took a sip of my tea. It tasted like weeds. "I understand he had a drinking problem."

"That's right. Even worse, Pete was a mean drunk. He'd get soused and set his sights on something he thought he ought to have. He didn't give a flip who was standing in his way. Fistfights, car wrecks, marriages falling apart . . . the consequences meant nothing to him."

"That must have been hard on his family," I said.

"Not just his family," Stella said. "It was hard on everyone around him. Stonebridge is a small town and Pete wreaked havoc around here. Plenty of people were just as happy when he disappeared. Excepting Betty, of course. She knew her son had lost his way, but she was always hopeful that Pete would find himself again."

"And Tyler? How did he feel about it? Were he and Pete close?"

"Not really. Not so's you'd notice anyway. It can't have been easy for Tyler, growing up in Peter's shadow. It wasn't his fault he wasn't born the favorite, but it was something he had to deal with. Tyler was a quiet child, the little boy standing in the background that you might not even notice when his brother was around. So I guess that's one good thing that came out of all of Pete's problems."

Faith tapped the toe of my boot with her paw. She

was looking for another cookie. Faith wasn't a spoiled dog, but she wanted to be. There was just a single shortbread cookie remaining. Stella looked on approvingly as I handed it over.

"One good thing?" I said.

"After Pete left, Tyler really stepped up. I guess you could say he came into his own. He's a whole new man now. Betty's spent the last five years pining for her lost son. I'd imagine Tyler spent the same amount of time thanking his lucky stars that Pete was gone."

Maybe that explained Tyler's dispassionate response to his older brother's death, I thought. Or maybe it gave him a motive for making sure that Pete never returned home.

"It was very nice to meet you, Stella," I said, rising to my feet. "Thank you for taking the time to talk to me."

"My pleasure. These days I'm happy to talk to anyone who comes by. Otherwise it's just me and the television."

She stood up and walked us to the door. "You want to talk to someone who knows what-all Pete got up to, you should go see his ex-wife, Penny. That woman will give you an earful whether you want one or not."

"Does she live in Stonebridge?"

"Yup. Born and raised here, just like the Dempseys. Her name is Penelope Whitten now. She took her maiden name back after the divorce. Not that that came as a surprise to anyone." Stella's lips curved upward in a smile. "Once she hears Pete's gone for good, she'll probably dance a jig right around the block."

"Stella sounds like a character," Sam said that night.

The kids were in bed and we were sitting in front of a fire and enjoying a glass of eggnog. The Poodles were spread out on the floor around us like a plush carpet. Bud was upstairs on Kevin's bed.

Some of the Christmas decorations had been put in place while I was away that afternoon. There was a wreath on the front door and an electric candle in each window. A length of pine roping had been wrapped around the banister in the front hall. Now the house was filled with that wonderful evergreen smell.

"But I'm not sure it's a good thing she recommended that you talk to Pete's ex-wife," Sam added. "Ex-wives can be dangerous."

Having met Sam's ex-wife, I was inclined to agree. On the other hand, I was an ex-wife as well. And Bob and I got along splendidly.

Well, most of the time anyway.

"Ex-wives also know where the bodies are buried," I pointed out. "Metaphorically speaking, of course."

"You're still concerned about what John Smith said, aren't you?"

I turned and faced Sam across the couch. "How can I not be? If Smith was right and Pete hadn't had a drink in months, then his death couldn't have been caused by a drunken stupor or intoxicated bumbling in the dark. The smell of gin on Pete's clothing? The empty bottles in his cabin? It looks like someone deliberately set out to mislead the police about what happened. Someone who had a hand in his death."

Neither one of us mentioned the word *murder*, but we were both thinking it.

"I'm not sure what kind of answers I can get from people who hadn't seen Pete in years," I said. "But I know I have to try."

Sam nodded. I wasn't sure whether the gesture was one of acquiescence or resignation. But then he raised his glass and tipped it in my direction, offering a brief salute. "Go get 'em. And let me know what you find out."

I rested my head on Sam's shoulder and wound my arm around his body, pulling us closer together. Perfect.

*   *   *

In my experience there was no point in calling people on the phone to ask them about something they might not want to discuss. Invariably they just hung up on me. When I appeared in person, however, I had much better luck.

Maybe that was because I looked like the elementary school teacher I actually was. Or maybe it was due to my winning personality. *Just kidding.* Most likely it was because I took Faith with me almost everywhere. And who could resist the obvious charms of a big, playful Standard Poodle?

Friday afternoon after school, Faith and I went back to Stonebridge. With the help of some mild internet stalking (thank you Facebook and Instagram) I not only had Penelope Whitten's address, I also knew that she was a stay-at-home mother of two adorable elementary school–age boys, and that she planned to spend the afternoon decorating the outside of her house.

Holy moly. If the average person ran into as many people with bad intentions as I do, they would know better than to put that much information out there for the taking. But considering Penelope's lack of internet discretion, I could only guess that the worst guy she'd ever run across was her ex-husband, Pete.

Her house was smaller than the Dempsey home and it was located closer to the center of town. The Cape

Cod–style home was painted light blue with white trim, and it sat up near the road on a narrow lot. A row of midsize bushes, each one trimmed into a neat square, flanked either side of the front door.

As advertised, Penelope was out in the front yard. At least, I assumed it was she, since the woman I saw was holding a giant ball of Christmas lights that she was attempting—not very successfully—to untangle. As I parked along the curb and got out, the woman lifted her head and glanced my way. Her hair was tucked up into a red knit cap, exposing an unlined forehead, a slender nose, and cheeks that were rosy from the cold. She would have been pretty except for the ferocious scowl on her face.

"Maybe I can help," I offered.

Since I wouldn't be going far, I had rolled down the windows on the passenger side of the car. As I walked across the yard, Faith stuck her head out to watch the proceedings. She was just as eager to see what would happen next as I was.

"Sure, why not? Four hands have to be better than two." The woman shrugged. "I guess you must be Melanie?"

"Um, yes." Sharon had told me this was a town where everybody knew everyone else's business, but even so, that was fast. "And you're Penelope?"

"Penny, please. The only one who called me Penelope

was Pete. He was a huge fan of Homer." She yanked on either end of the ball of lights and when they separated slightly, passed one side over to me. "You know, the *Odyssey*?"

"Your husband compared you to Odysseus's faithful, long-suffering wife?" I teased a plug free of the tangle and began to gently work backwards.

"I know. What a joke, right?" Penny smiled grimly. "I didn't have anywhere near twenty years of patience for my errant husband's antics. Half that was more than enough for me."

Since she knew who I was, I assumed that Penny must know the rest of the message I'd come to Stonebridge to deliver. She must have read my mind, because Penny didn't look up from the skein of lights in her hands when she said, "Yes, I heard that Pete died recently. And that he froze to death, which is ironic considering how much he loved cold weather. So you don't have to stand there worrying about breaking it to me. That news was all over town in ten minutes yesterday."

I separated out a single strand of lights, straightened them carefully, then set them down on the dry front steps. "You don't sound terribly broken up about what happened."

"I'm upset for Peter and Christopher's sake. They're my kids, and now they'll never have a chance to get to

Chapter
Ten

For a few minutes, I applied myself to the task at hand. Thanks to the number of knotted shoelaces I've had to deal with over the years, I'm quite adept at untangling things. Even a mess of lights that looked as though they'd been tossed willy-nilly into a box at the end of the previous holiday season.

"I guess you think that sounds harsh," Penny said eventually.

"I didn't know your ex-husband," I replied. "So it's not up to me to judge."

"Pete was a drunk. That pretty much sums up all you need to know."

I pulled another strand of lights free and set them aside. "He must have had some redeeming qualities. After all, you married him."

"He did," Penny admitted. "Back in the days when

know their father again. But maybe that never would have worked out anyway."

Now Penny did look up. The expression on her face was fierce. "You want to know how I really feel about my ex-husband's death? I'm glad it happened. That rat bastard had it coming."

he thought alcohol was for social drinking. Before it became a crutch he used to deal with things he didn't want to think about. Before it took over his life and turned him into a man I could barely recognize."

"I'm sorry," I said. "That must have been terrible for you."

"It was." Penny's fingers clenched around the wires in her hands. I hoped the tension in her distracted grasp didn't snap off any lights. "But I'm not the only one whose life was negatively impacted by Pete's behavior. He screwed over his business partners. He shafted his best friend. He even cheated on his mistress."

When I bit back a startled laugh, Penny looked up. "Yes, I knew about her. In case you're wondering, people who drink too much aren't any good at keeping secrets."

"No, I guess not," I said.

Penny wasn't making any headway with her lights at all. I laid my last unknotted strand on the steps with the others and took the remaining lights out of her hands. She seemed relieved to hand them over.

"I didn't deserve to be treated the way Pete treated me," Penny said grimly. "None of us did. Pete had a choice and he chose the booze. Repeatedly. Over his family. Over his career. The drinking was more important to him than anything. He could have stopped, but he didn't."

I thought back to what John Smith had said. I wondered if Pete had been planning to return to his hometown and his family once he was certain he had things under control.

Penny picked up a strand of tangle-free lights. She began to drape it around the bush nearest the front door. There was more vigor than artistry to her application.

"Pete did stop drinking," I said.

She glanced at me over her shoulder. "No. He didn't."

"A friend of his named John Smith told me Pete hadn't had a drink in several months."

Penny just shrugged. "I don't know anyone named John Smith. But Pete called here a couple of weeks ago. He told me some cockamamy story about wanting to make things right. As if I would believe that."

"Maybe he meant it," I said.

"*Meaning it* isn't the problem," Penny growled. "Pete always *meant it* when he said he was going to stop. In that moment, he was sure he was telling the truth. Then he always relapsed anyway. After a while I realized it was safer not to believe anything he told me."

"John said he was going to meetings. That he'd stayed sober—"

"So what?" Penny rounded on me. "So some stranger thinks that Pete was sober? Big deal. I was Pete's *wife*. I was living with the guy and I didn't always know. At least not in the beginning, when Pete was still good at hiding what he didn't want people to see. He was great at sounding sincere and making promises."

She gulped in a deep breath of air. Her face crumpled. For a moment I thought she might cry. Then she gathered herself together and said, "And you know what else he was good at? *Breaking* promises. But you don't have to believe me about that. Talk to his ex-partners, Owen Strunk and Larry Potts at Streamline Search. They'll tell you the same thing."

Faith and I left Penny to finish putting up her lights and drove to Streamline Search in downtown Stonebridge. The company was housed in a two-story brick building with a parking lot out front. Streamline's offices were on the ground floor. I attached a leash to Faith's collar and walked her beside me into the lobby.

A receptionist was sitting behind a low counter that was decorated with festive cardboard candy canes. Christmas music filled the air. The woman looked up and smiled. Then she saw Faith by my side. Her double take was almost comical.

"Is that a service dog?" she asked.

"No. But she's a very obedient pet. I'm here to see either Larry Potts or Owen Strunk. Are they available?"

"Let me check." She reached for her phone. "Do you have an appointment?"

"I'm afraid I don't. I'm only in town briefly this afternoon. Penny Whitten recommended that I come and talk to them."

"Penny sent you. Okay." That seemed to bolster my credibility. "Let me take you into the conference room and I'll go get Larry." Once again, she stared at Faith dubiously. "Is she an emotional support dog?"

"No." I gave her a wide smile. "Just a great companion. Would you like to see her do some tricks?"

Faith tipped her head to one side and stared up at me balefully. Her message was clear: *Tricks are beneath my dignity.*

I sent back a message of my own: *Humor me, this is working. Unless you'd rather go outside and wait in the car?*

Faith just sighed.

"No, I don't need to see any tricks," the woman said brightly. "If the two of you would please follow me?"

She led us down the hallway to a glass-walled conference room. A long rectangular table in the middle of the room was surrounded by chairs. I took a seat at the end near the door. Faith lay down on the floor beside me. We didn't have long to wait.

Larry came striding into the room first. He'd barely finished introducing himself before Owen followed. He paused to close the door behind him.

Both men were in their forties, but that was all they had in common. Larry was tall and slim, dressed in a suit and tie that fit him impeccably. With his carefully styled hair and dark-framed glasses, he projected an image of stability and authority.

Owen, on the other hand, walked toward me bouncing on the balls of his feet. He was already smiling before he reached out to pump my hand heartily. If he'd worn a tie to work that morning, it was gone now. As was his jacket. His shirtsleeves were rolled back, revealing a watch on his wrist that looked complicated enough to launch rockets.

"Nice dog," Owen said, sliding Faith a glance as he grabbed a seat at the table. "That's some hairdo."

Long retired from the show ring, Faith was wearing the easy-to-care-for kennel trim, with a short blanket of dense curls covering her entire body. Only her face, her feet, and the base of her tail were clipped and I'd left a large pompon on the end of her tail. If Owen was impressed by her looks, it was a good thing I hadn't brought along Augie, who was in a show trim.

"Owen . . . let's concentrate, shall we?" Larry ignored Faith and turned to me. "You said that Penny sent you. What is this in reference to?"

"Pete Dempsey."

Larry's lips pursed distastefully. "We heard that he

had died. I understand his body was found under a tree in some woods."

"I'm the one who found him," I said.

"Ouch." Owen grimaced. "That can't have been good."

"It wasn't."

Larry declined to offer sympathy. Instead he remained on point. "What do you want from us?"

"I'm trying to understand what happened," I said. "The police think Pete's death was an accident. I'm not sure they're right."

"I see," Larry replied. "Do you suspect that someone from Pete's sordid past might have wanted to harm him? Perhaps someone like his former business partners?"

Owen grinned at that. I merely shrugged.

"What I know so far is that Pete disappeared from Stonebridge approximately five years ago after developing a severe drinking problem," I said. "I gather he'd left a trail of destruction in his wake. Pete ended up in Wilton, where he was homeless and living on handouts. At some point recently, he decided to stop drinking—"

"I sincerely doubt that," said Larry. "Pete's problem with alcohol wasn't just that he drank. It was that he loved everything about drinking. Getting, having, and consuming alcohol became the only thing he cared about. Certainly it was more important to him than the welfare of this company."

Owen bounded up out of his chair. He walked around the room as he spoke. "Pete had a support system of family and friends here in Stonebridge. I can't count the number of times we stepped in—sometimes singly, sometimes together—and tried to get help for him. But Pete didn't want to be helped. Pardon me for being skeptical, but if Pete could have controlled his addiction to alcohol, he'd have stopped drinking a long time ago."

"His behavior must have played havoc with your business," I said.

"The three of us started this company together and built it from the ground up," Larry told me. "Pete's drinking cost us clients and it cost us goodwill in the industry. Indeed, his reckless disregard for industry standards and practices nearly took us under."

"And then there was the money Pete helped himself to on the sly—" Owen muttered. A sharp look from his partner caused him to stop speaking.

"I don't think Melanie needs to hear about that," Larry said smoothly. "Suffice it to say, it was a good thing that Pete parted company with us when he did."

"That happened before he left Stonebridge?"

"Yes. Probably two months earlier. We dissolved our partnership and Owen and I bought out his share of the business. Much of the money we paid him went to Penny for the children."

"We hoped that losing his place in the company would serve as a wake-up call," Owen said. "Instead, it only seemed to increase his booze budget for a few weeks. And then suddenly he was gone."

"And you didn't know where he went or how he could be reached?" I asked.

Owen and Larry looked at each other. Both men shook their heads.

"It's not as if anyone wanted to go after him," Owen told me. "By that point, Pete had burned every bridge he had in this town."

"And you haven't heard from him since?"

The two men shared another look. Larry sat perfectly still in his chair. Owen was fidgety on his feet. I got the distinct impression that an unspoken message passed between them. Something they didn't want me to know.

"We haven't heard from Pete," Larry said firmly. "And I, for one, haven't given him a second thought. Leaving Stonebridge behind was his choice. If that was what he wanted, I was happy to oblige him."

Owen paused beside my chair. He squatted down and ruffled his hands in Faith's ears. Without looking up, he said, "You might want to talk to Olivia Brent."

Larry frowned. "Owen, don't."

"Don't what?" I asked.

"It's none of our business."

"What isn't?" Now I was really curious.

"At one point, Pete and Olivia were quite friendly with each other," Owen said obliquely.

It only took a moment for understanding to dawn. "Olivia was his mistress," I said. "Penny told me there was someone else."

Larry looked shocked. "Penny told you that?"

Men. They always overestimated themselves and underestimated us.

"Did you think she didn't know?" I asked.

"I *hoped* she didn't know."

"Well, you were wrong." I gathered up my things and stood. "Where would I find Olivia Brent?"

"Probably at the gym," Owen told me. "Or running on the high school track after hours. That woman really knows how to take care of herself."

Larry still looked annoyed. "She won't be happy to hear from you."

Like that was anything new.

Faith hopped up and we headed for the door together.

"Whatever you do, don't tell her we sent you," Larry called after me.

"I wouldn't dream of it," I said.

Out in the lobby, the same Christmas music was still playing. The receptionist didn't seem to mind. She gave me a cheery wave.

"I hope you got everything you needed," she said.

Not yet, I thought. Not by a long shot. But I would. I'd make sure of that.

Chapter
Eleven

I was blissfully asleep on Saturday morning when the bed gave a sudden lurch and something small and solid bounced onto my stomach. *Bud*. Kevin—the little dog's partner-in-crime—wasn't far behind.

"We're getting a Christmas tree today!" he crowed happily as he climbed up onto the bed. "Get up! Get up!"

Sam rolled over groggily. Lucky man, no errant dogs or children had landed on him. "What time is it?"

"Time to get up," Kev informed him. "Time to go chop down a tree."

"What's all the noise about?" Davey appeared in the bedroom doorway.

Behind him in the hallway were Eve, Tar, and Augie: a Standard Poodle honor guard. Faith and Raven had been asleep on the floor in our room, but now they were up as well.

Everyone looked at Sam and me expectantly. As if they thought we had all the answers. Good luck with that.

"Last night someone told Kevin that we were going tree shopping today." Sam answered Davey's question.

Oh. That might have been me.

Maybe I'd been feeling a little guilty about how much I'd been away this past week. Maybe I'd thought that a fun family outing would be just the thing to restore myself to everyone's good graces. Picking out the right tree, bringing it home and trimming it, had seemed like the perfect activity for us to enjoy together. Too bad I'd overlooked my younger son's rampant enthusiasm for All Things Christmas.

"Good one, Mom," Davey muttered. He didn't even need to be told who was responsible for the early morning wake-up call.

"After we get the Christmas tree, Santa Claus comes," Kev said happily.

"Not right away." I grabbed him, rolled him into my arms, and began to tickle below his ribs. "Once the tree is up, you still have three more weeks to wait."

"Don't want to wait." He tried to push out his lower lip in a pout, but he was laughing too hard to make it work. Instead he squealed and thrust himself away—only to be snatched up by Sam, who smothered him in a big, soft pillow. That led to more squealing.

Bouncing up and down with the movement on the bed, Bud began to bark. After a few seconds Tar and Augie joined in. The two dogs slipped past Davey and leaped up onto the mattress to join the fray.

"You people are all nuts." Davey was still standing in the doorway. He knew better than to come close enough for one of us to grab him.

"*You people*," Sam scoffed. "We're your family. And now that you're a teenager it's our duty to embarrass you. It's in the parents' manual."

"Nuts," Davey repeated. He shook his head and turned away. "I'm going to let the dogs out."

"Good idea," I said.

Everyone in the vicinity understood the word *out*. Even Tar. There was a flurry of scrambling feet and jostling bodies, as an abrupt mass exodus emptied the room. Kevin scooted off the bed and went flying after them. With two boys and six dogs pounding down the stairs, it sounded like someone had turned a herd of buffalo loose in the house.

Sam and I looked at each other. *Alone at last.*

"You don't suppose Davey will let Kev go outside too?" Sam said thoughtfully.

"Of course not. Kev's in his pajamas. There's snow on the ground . . ." I stopped and considered. Then I

jumped out of bed and went running after them.
"Davey . . . *wait!*"

Mid-morning when we arrived at Haney's Holiday
Home, business was hopping. Two cars with trees
fastened to their roofs were exiting the property as
we approached. Once inside, we saw several more vehicles parked in the small lot.

"Kudos to Frank," Sam said as we headed up the
steps to the office. "I was skeptical when I first saw
the place, but it looks like he's making a go of this."

I'd have expected my brother to be on hand on this
busy Saturday morning—if only so that he could gloat
about proving his doubters wrong. But when we entered the building, Frank was nowhere to be seen. Instead, Claire was standing behind the counter and
Bob appeared to be taking an order from a customer.

"Merry Christmas!" Claire sang out a cheery
greeting.

Tall and slender, she still managed to look svelte
dressed in a bulky holiday sweater. An image of
Rudolph the Reindeer, complete with 3-D antlers
and a blinking red nose, covered her from collarbone
to waist. That improbable article of clothing was
matched with a green elf cap, perched atop Claire's
long, dark hair.

"Doesn't this place look great?" she asked.

"Fabulous," I agreed.

The decorations I'd seen early in the week—garlands of golden tinsel, shiny ornaments, and braided Christmas ribbons—were now hanging on the walls and draped around the counter. The inflatable Santa Claus had been blown up and positioned in the middle of the room. Struck by the chill breeze when we opened the door, he bobbed back and forth in place. The movement made him look as though he was waving hello to incoming customers.

I scooted around behind the counter to give Claire a quick hug. "You've done a fantastic job here."

"Not me," she said. "I wish I could take the credit, but mostly it belongs to Frank."

"Speaking of my little brother, where is he? I thought he'd be here today having a ball."

Bob finished dealing with his customer, then turned to talk to us. "Frank's over at The Bean Counter. Pre-Christmas, we do plenty of extra business there too. It's not like we can slack off at our principle location for the sake of a seasonal fling here. For the next month, he and I will be running ragged trying to keep both places functioning at peak performance."

"Christmas season is a slow time of year for me," Sam said. He worked freelance designing computer software, mostly for long-term clients. "If you want, I'd be happy to pitch in."

"Seriously? That would be great." Bob clapped Sam hard on the shoulder, a gesture of male solidarity that has always looked more painful than gratifying to me. At least they hadn't bumped fists or hips.

"I can help after school and on weekends," said Davey.

"Me too," Kevin offered. He hates to be left out of anything.

"You guys are terrific. Don't be surprised if I take you up on that." Bob's gaze swung my way. "How about you, Mel? You must have a few hours to spare for the family business."

Before I could reply the office door opened, admitting a blast of cold air along with Aunt Peg and Snowball. The Maltese was sporting a new collar and jaunty red leash. When Aunt Peg paused to stamp the snow off her boots on the doormat, Snowball ran ahead into the room. Aunt Peg dropped the lead and the Maltese made a beeline for Kevin who was sitting on the floor.

"Greetings!" Aunt Peg said heartily. "This looks like a lively gathering. What did I miss?"

"Dad said that Sam and I can come and help run this place," Davey announced. "Isn't that cool?"

"Very cool," Aunt Peg agreed. "I've always said you were a useful child." Useful people were her favorite kind. She turned and looked at me. "And you?"

"I have plenty to tell you," I said. "Maybe I can recap while we go pick out our tree?"

After our experience the week before, none of us wanted to venture very far into the woods surrounding the buildings. That hardly limited our choices, however. There were still dozens of pine trees for us to inspect and evaluate.

Sam and the boys went racing ahead through the snow, examining and discarding numerous options in their quest to find the perfect Christmas tree to grace our living room. Aunt Peg and I followed slowly behind as I brought her up to speed on all that had happened since the last time we'd spoken. She had handed Snowball's leash to Kevin and the Maltese was bounding happily through the low drifts. When the boys paused to look at a tree, the little white dog would lower his head and push his nose through the powder until his face was coated with a froth of white crystals. Aunt Peg watched his antics with a bemused smile on her face.

"It does seem like a shame," she said when I'd finished my report.

"What does?"

"That a man is dead and nobody appears to be mourning his loss."

"I gather that was Pete's own fault. By the time he disappeared from Stonebridge, he'd left behind more enemies than friends."

"Hey Mom, hurry up!" Davey called back. "I think we've found it!"

The tree my family had settled upon was a glorious Douglas fir. It stood more than six feet tall, was dark green in color, and had a full, symmetrical silhouette. Best of all, it smelled heavenly. I drew in a deep breath and was flooded with memories of Christmases past.

"Great choice," I said. "It's perfect."

Sam was carrying a chain saw he'd picked up in the office. Davey had dragged along a sled to transport the tree back to the parking area. It wasn't long before the six of us were on our way out of the woods. Snowball had been returned to Aunt Peg's care and Kevin was riding on the sled with the tree.

"Faster!" Kev whooped gleefully. "You guys are too slow!"

"Maybe that's because you're too heavy," Davey told him.

"No." Kev shook his head. "You just need to try harder."

Sam and the boys deposited the sled beside the SUV. As they went into the office to get some rope to tie up the tree, a small pickup truck came bumping up the driveway. Aunt Peg and I had been about to follow the rest of the family inside when the truck pulled into a parking space and John Smith got out.

Abruptly I stopped and turned back. Aunt Peg followed my lead.

"Who's that?" she asked as he came walking toward us.

"John Smith," I told her.

"Excellent," she said under her breath.

His long strides made short work of the distance between us. A knit cap was pulled low over Smith's forehead. His mouth, below the dark moustache, was drawn into a thin line.

"I just came by to tell you I was right," he said.

"About what?"

"Pete wasn't drunk. Not even close. There wasn't any alcohol in his system at all."

"How very interesting," said Aunt Peg.

Smith's gaze swung her way. "And you are?"

"Peg Turnbull. Innocent bystander."

My foot, I thought.

John Smith didn't look terribly impressed either. He looked back at me. "I just thought you should know."

"Thank you," I said. "Are the police aware of that?"

"They're the ones who told me. Guy named Officer Shiner?"

I shrugged. "We barely exchanged names with the officers who were here. Their level of interest didn't seem to require it. Has that changed now?"

"I hope so," Smith replied. "I told them Pete was off the sauce. They didn't believe me any more than you did." He turned and started to walk away.

"His family doesn't believe it either," I said.

Smith spun back around. "You found them?"

"Yes. His name was Peter Charles Dempsey and he came from Stonebridge. He disappeared five years ago and nobody from there has seen him since."

Smith frowned. The downturned moustache gave him a ferocious look. "That can't be right."

"Why not?" asked Aunt Peg.

"Pete's been trying to put his life back together."

"So you said," I agreed.

"Part of the process involved contacting people he'd hurt in the past. Apologizing, trying to make amends. Pete had started doing that over the last month or so."

I shook my head. That didn't jibe with what I'd been told. "Almost everyone I spoke to said they hadn't heard from him in years. His high school sweetheart told me that people had tried to find Pete after he left Stonebridge. But nobody knew where he'd disappeared to."

"They *should* have known," Smith insisted.

"I understand Pete wasn't the most stable character," Aunt Peg said gently. "Maybe he was lying to you about his actions."

"Or maybe the people you talked to were the ones who were lying," Smith replied. "I got the impression Pete had ticked off a lot of folks in his former life."

"He did," I agreed. "People said they were happy to be rid of him when he left."

"That's precisely my point."

Aunt Peg nodded. "I like the way your mind works, Mr. Smith. You're thinking that one of Pete's former associates might have wanted to be rid of him permanently, aren't you?"

Smith eyed us both. "You're darn right I am. Aren't you?"

Chapter
Twelve

Sunday I went back to Stonebridge. How could I resist?

I wondered if Olivia Brent went to the gym on weekends. Pete's business partner, Owen, had implied that she worked out every day. In December, that probably meant somewhere indoors. I figured that checking out the only fitness center in town was worth a try. Because sometimes you just get lucky. And indeed, at the beginning of the day good fortune seemed to be on my side.

I stopped at the gym's front desk and presented myself as an old friend of Olivia's, hoping to surprise her. The attendant smiled cheerfully and directed me around the corner to the weight room. Only one person was currently inside. A petite, elfin woman—blond hair scrunched up in a ponytail on top of her head, corded muscles glistening with sweat—was lifting an implement the size of a small couch.

Seriously, I was impressed.

As I lingered in the doorway, Olivia lowered the bar, then dropped it with a small bounce on the mat at her feet. She reached around behind her and grabbed a water bottle. After taking a long swallow, she screwed the cap back on, then glared across the room at me and said, "What are you looking at?"

That got my feet moving. "Olivia Brent?" I made my way carefully around the various instruments of torture between us.

One brow lifted delicately. "Who wants to know?"

"I'm Melanie Travis. I was told I might find you here."

"So you're Melanie." Olivia didn't look surprised to see me. "Where's the dog? I heard there was going to be one."

Small-town gossip, you had to love it. And I'd thought the dog show grapevine was efficient.

"Just so you know," she added, "I don't like dogs."

"I'm sorry," I said. I meant that sincerely. Anyone who didn't like dogs was missing out on one of the great joys in life. "But Faith stayed home today."

"Dogs should stay home every day. That way they won't bother people." Her emphasis on the last two words made it clear that my presence was every bit as much of an annoyance as Faith's would have been.

"I was hoping we could talk for a few minutes," I said.

"And I was hoping for an uninterrupted workout." Olivia took another drink of water. "Oh what the hell, why not? I know you've seen everyone else. If you'd missed me, I'd have probably felt slighted."

I opened my mouth to speak. She held up a hand to forestall my first question.

"Not here. First I need a shower. You can meet me in the juice bar in fifteen minutes. Grab a table and order me a raspberry banana smoothie. Grande, with extra fruit."

"Got it." If that was the price of Olivia's cooperation, I was probably getting off easy.

The juice bar was on the other side of the building. I ordered two smoothies and sat down to wait. I'd chosen a table from which I could see the gym's front door because I was half-afraid that Olivia might ditch me and use the fifteen minutes to give herself a head start. But twelve minutes later she came gliding into the juice bar, tossed a duffel bag on the floor next to the table, and slid into the chair opposite me.

"So Pete's dead," she said. "Tell me about it."

While I did that, Olivia downed half her smoothie in several quick gulps. She struck me as the kind of woman who did everything with gusto. In other circumstances, I would have hoped we'd become friends.

"Well, that's gruesome," she said when I'd finished. "Poor Pete. I wouldn't wish an end like that on anyone."

"I understand that you and he had a relationship," I said obliquely.

Olivia grinned at my choice of words. "Yeah, the kind of relationship that broke up my marriage. Pete and I were sleeping together. It lasted two years. Is that what you wanted to hear?"

She'd clearly been hoping to shock me. If so, she'd have to try a little harder than that. "Actually, I was wondering whether you'd seen Pete recently."

"No. Not in years." Olivia seemed to be taken aback by the question. "What do you mean?"

"Pete was trying to get his life back together. He'd entered a program to help him quit drinking. According to his sponsor, he'd been sober for three months. Pete was getting in touch with people whom he felt he'd wronged in the past and asking for their forgiveness."

"Well, that wouldn't have been me." Olivia took another gulp of her drink. "What Pete and I did together might have been wrong by society's standards, but we both went into the affair with our eyes wide open. And for a while, we had a blast together. If Pete had tried to apologize for *that*, I'd have been offended, you know?"

I didn't actually, but I nodded anyway. "Were you surprised to hear of his death?"

"Sad to say, not really. The liquor, which I'm sure everyone has talked about endlessly until you're tired of listening to it, wasn't his only problem. Pete always had his demons."

"Like what?" My smoothie was strawberry avocado. The barista had recommended it. I hadn't been sure that the flavors would work together, but the result was delicious.

"Oh you know, just stuff."

"Problems with his marriage?"

Olivia snorted derisively. "Considering who you're talking to, I'd say that's a given, wouldn't you?"

Point taken.

"His job?" I asked.

Olivia waved a hand through the air, dismissing my second guess. "When Pete and I were together, he was living a pretty cushy life. At that point his dark days were few and far between. Whatever was bothering him was something he'd buried pretty deep."

"But he never told you what it was?"

"He never said anything about it at all. Pete hated discussing private stuff. Besides, when he and I had a chance to see each other, we had *much* better things to do than sit around and talk about the past."

"So if Pete didn't talk to you about his problems, who did?"

"Kenny."

That wasn't a name I'd heard before. "Who's Kenny?"

"Pete's best friend from the time they were little kids. The two of them grew up on the same block. They went to the same schools. Those guys did everything together when they were young. Pete was the quarterback on the football team, Kenny was a wide receiver. Pete started Streamline here in Stonebridge, Kenny sells insurance on the other side of town. If you want to know stuff about Pete's early life, you should talk to Kenny. In fact, I'm surprised you haven't already done so."

When she put it like that, I was too. I'd been in Stonebridge for most of the week, so how come this was the first time I was hearing about him?

"Of course, he probably isn't going to want to talk to you," Olivia added.

"Why is that?"

"The two of them didn't part company on the best of terms."

Like I hadn't heard that before. "What went wrong?"

"Same old story, I guess. Kenny wasn't the only one of Pete's buddies who got scammed, but he took it more personally than most. Pete came to him with a surefire business idea. Said the two of them would be partners; he just needed some money for start-up costs. Pete told Kenny they'd be rolling in dough in six months."

"I assume that didn't happen?" I said.

"Not even close. Probably there was never any kind of deal in the works. By that time whatever money Pete managed to score was going straight into the bottle. Kenny certainly should have known better. But Pete could be very convincing when he wanted to be. And Kenny trusted his best friend to do right by him."

"I can understand why he would be bitter. That sounds like a terrible betrayal." I considered for a minute then added, "But what I don't understand is why Kenny would talk about Pete's private problems with you."

Olivia polished off the last of her smoothie and stood up. She crossed the room in three quick strides and flicked the empty plastic cup into a recycling bin. "I thought you knew," she said.

"Knew what?"

"In Stonebridge everyone has the dirt on everyone else's lives. I just assumed someone would have told you."

I hated to ask again but I couldn't help it. "Told me *what*?"

Olivia swept her duffel bag up off the floor and hooked the strap over her shoulder. "Kenny wasn't just Pete's best friend. He's also my ex-husband."

I think my mouth was still hanging open when she disappeared through the doorway.

In a town the size of Stonebridge it wasn't difficult to locate a guy named Kenny who sold insurance. I didn't expect to find him in his office on a Sunday, but like most salesmen he was eager to be accessible to potential clients. Kenny listed alternate phone numbers where he could be reached 24/7. So I gave him a call on his cell phone.

Kenny picked up after just two rings. His ex-wife had spent the morning at the gym. Kenny was at a dog park. That was a lucky break. Maybe he and I could bond over our mutual love of dogs.

Kenny told me he had a Great Dane named Rufus. I told him I had five Standard Poodles. He asked me if I was interested in discussing liability insurance. He informed me that someone with multiple large dogs ought to have an umbrella policy in place. I said I was interested in discussing his former good buddy, Pete Dempsey.

That was when Kenny hung up.

A brief internet search supplied directions to Stonebridge's only dog park. When I arrived, there were six dogs racing around the large enclosure. A harlequin Great Dane was playing tag with a Border Collie that looked agile enough to run rings around him. A brindle

Boxer appeared ready to join their game. I was betting that the Dane's name was Rufus.

Five minutes of watching from my car allowed me to match most of the dogs with their owners. Kenny was tall and skinny with watery blue eyes and a prominent nose. Dressed in a woolen peacoat, standing with his shoulders hunched forward and his hands shoved deep in the pockets of his jeans, he looked like he was freezing. I got out of my car and ambled over.

"Go away," he said as I approached.

The hostility in his tone caused several nearby dog owners to turn and have a look at us. As if by consensus, they followed his dictate and removed themselves from the vicinity. I didn't think that was what Kenny had in mind.

"You don't even know what I'm going to say yet," I told him.

"I can guess," he mumbled.

"Go ahead."

"Go ahead and what?"

"Guess," I said. I was standing right in front of him now.

Kenny scowled. "I'm not playing your game."

"No games. I'm just trying to figure out who disliked your old friend Pete enough to want to kill him."

Kenny lifted his fingers to his lips and gave a loud

whistle. Rufus, still busy playing with his friends, ignored him. "It wasn't me."

"I didn't think it was," I said.

That got his attention. "Why not?"

I opted for honesty. "If you didn't murder him five
years ago when he swindled you out of money and
slept with your wife, you probably weren't going to
do it now."

"Then why are you here?"

"Maybe I'm hoping you have some ideas. You're
the man who knew Pete better than anyone. Did he
have any enemies?"

Kenny barked out a laugh. "That's rich. Would you
like a list?"

"Sure. Or you can start by telling me what you told
Olivia. She said Pete had his demons. I'm wondering
what they were."

"That stuff's old news." When he blew out a breath,
condensation swirled in the air between us. "I'm not
going to rehash what went on in high school. Certainly
not with *you*."

"I thought you might be interested in seeing justice
served."

"I can't imagine why. Will justice return my money?
Will it bring back my marriage?"

When I didn't reply right away, Kenny shook his
head. "Yeah, I didn't think so."

Rufus came wandering by. Kenny reached out and snagged the Great Dane's collar. He pulled a leather lead out of his pocket and snapped it on. The pair started to walk away, then Kenny stopped and looked back. "If you figure out who did it, let me know. I'd like to buy the guy a beer."

Chapter
Thirteen

At least my trip to the dog park hadn't been a total loss.

Though Kenny had been determined not to talk to me, an interesting tidbit had still slipped out. *I'm not going to rehash what went on in high school,* he'd said. Pete's past life encompassed a lot of years. Now I was pretty sure my search had just been narrowed down considerably.

I had to wait until Tuesday to get back to Stonebridge again. In the intervening day-and-a-half, we brought our new Christmas tree into the house and decorated it, I managed to sneak out for some surreptitious Christmas shopping, and the Poodle pack did their best to make me feel guilty that none of the running around I was doing included them. That led to numerous long walks around the neighborhood and the distribution of more peanut butter biscuits than were strictly necessary. Aunt Peg wasn't the only one who knew how to play me like a harp.

Monday at school my ability to concentrate was sadly lacking. In my defense, I wasn't the only one. Now that Christmas was almost upon us, half the students I tutored had already left for holiday vacations in far-flung locales. The other half were dreaming of the parties they planned to attend or the presents Santa would be leaving beneath their Christmas trees. If any serious schoolwork was being performed during this lead-up to the holiday, I certainly wasn't aware of it.

By the time I left Howard Academy on Tuesday afternoon, I felt nothing but a sense of relief that I was finally on my way back to Pete's hometown. I had a hunch that I was closing in on something important and I was hoping that Pete's high school girlfriend, Sharon LaRue, might be able to help me figure out what it was.

Planning ahead that morning, I'd left Faith at home with Sam and the other Poodles for company. That seemed like a better alternative than making her sit in the high school parking lot again.

This time when I walked in the school's front door, I knew where I was going. I didn't pass a single person on my way to the assistant principal's office. Nor was anyone sitting at the outer desk. Apparently Howard Academy wasn't the only school dealing with the effects of the upcoming holiday.

Sharon LaRue's office door was slightly ajar. I knocked lightly and waited until she looked up from a paper she'd been studying and acknowledged my presence. Today her tawny hair was loose around her shoulders. The style made her look both younger and prettier. A wool sweater dress hugged her generous curves.

Sharon had a pair of reading glasses perched on her nose. She removed them and set them carefully to one side of her desk before greeting me with a half-smile.

"Melanie Travis," she said. An ability to remember names was probably helpful in her position. "I didn't expect to see you again."

"Do you mind if I come in?"

"No, but I'm a little pressed for time." She glanced at a clock on the wall. "I can spare ten minutes though. What's this about?"

"As you may know, I've been speaking with some of Pete Dempsey's former friends and family."

Sharon nodded. "Pretty much everyone in town is aware of that. I have to admit I'm not sure what you hope to achieve. Pete left Stonebridge a long time ago. Nobody here has any desire to dredge those memories back up."

"It appears that Pete's death may not have been an accident," I said.

It took Sharon a moment to absorb what I'd said. Then her body went utterly still. "What are you talking about?"

"When Pete died, there was no alcohol in his system. And according to a current friend of his, Pete hadn't had a drink in months. As part of the program he'd joined to get sober, Pete had been making contact with people from his past."

Sharon shook her head. "I can hardly believe that. This is the first I've heard of it."

"So he didn't attempt to get in touch with you?"

"Heavens no. Why would he? Our relationship ended years before his problems began. Pete and I had both long since moved on."

A picture was sitting on the corner of Sharon's desk. She reached over and turned the frame around so I could see photograph within. An attractive man with grizzled gray hair and a wide smile was standing with his arm around a younger woman who was mugging for the camera.

"That's my husband, Steve, with our daughter Amy," Sharon told me. "Steve and I got married our freshman year in college. Our parents thought we were too young to know what we wanted, but it will be twenty-three happy years next June. So you see, I was lucky. When Pete broke up with me, I met the love of my life. If he'd attempted to get in touch with me after all this time, the only thing I would have had to say to him is *thank you*."

"Most people in Stonebridge don't share your equanimity," I said. "A couple of them have alluded to something that might have happened to Pete a long time ago. Maybe while he was here in school?"

"Something like what?"

"I don't know. That's why I came to see you. Last time we spoke you implied that Pete had led a charmed life when he was young. But nobody's life is perfect, especially not in high school. I'm wondering if something could have happened that you didn't mention. Some kind of unresolved issue that might have plagued him later."

Sharon thought for a minute before answering. "There was one thing. Not an issue, exactly. More like a rivalry. You met Pete's brother, Tyler."

"Just briefly," I said. "He wasn't eager to talk to me."

"That's not surprising. Tyler was never eager to get involved with anything that had to do with Pete. Those brothers were always competitive and unfortunately for Tyler, he was usually on the losing end of things. I remember when he was a sophomore, he went out for the football team. As you can see, this isn't a big school. It's not like our sports teams can afford to turn away anyone who wants to play, you know?"

I nodded.

"Pete was a senior by then and he was the quarterback. He made it clear to the coach that he wasn't going to play on any team that included his little brother. He didn't even want Tyler sitting on the bench. He insisted his brother be relegated to the stands with the parents, the nerds, and rest of the kids who couldn't hack it."

"That terrible," I said.

"I totally agree with you. But that's how those two were with one another. They fought over everything, no matter how trivial." Sharon pushed back her chair and stood. "Pete's disappearance was the best thing that ever happened to Tyler. Even if it's by default, he's the favorite son now."

Sharon walked past me and headed for the door. I turned and followed.

"I guess you heard that their mother isn't doing well?"

"Yes, you mentioned that before."

"I don't think poor Betty has long to live. And, of course, the news of Pete's death must have come as a huge blow to her."

"If Pete had tried to contact his mother," I asked, "would Tyler have given him access?"

Sharon frowned. "Truthfully, I don't know the answer to that. You'll have to ask him yourself."

"If you had to guess?" I pressed.

Sharon leaned toward me. Her voice dropped to a whisper. "Pete and Tyler were Betty's only children and their father has been dead for years. So now there's an inheritance to consider too. Under those circumstances, do I think Tyler would have allowed Pete back in their mother's life? No way in hell do I see that happening."

*   *   *

I left the high school and drove to the Dempseys' house, planning to have a conversation with whomever answered the door—Tyler or Betty, either one was fine with me.

Since the last time I'd been to Meadow Lane, Christmas decorations had gone up around the neighborhood. The houses on either side of the Dempsey home had fairy lights on their eaves, ornate wreaths on their front doors, and pine roping wrapped around their mailbox posts. Compared to the holiday festivity that surrounded it, the house I parked in front of looked plain. Almost somber.

A gauzy curtain in a front window flicked open as I got out of my car. It fell back into place when I was on the brick walkway. Once again, Tyler Dempsey didn't wait for me to reach the door before he opened it and stepped outside.

"You shouldn't have come back here," he said.

I gazed up at him. Sunlight glanced off the snow around me and I had to lift my hand to shade my eyes. "I've been talking to people about your brother."

Tyler grimaced slightly. "I suppose you think I should care about that."

"In your place, I would."

"That's hardly relevant, is it? You and I know nothing about one another. I doubt we have anything in common."

"I was hoping we could talk." I started up the steps.

Tyler folded his arms across his chest. "I will not have you in this house."

"Fine," I snapped. "Then out here. Maybe you'd like to get a coat?"

He reached inside around the doorframe. There must have been a coat rack there because a leather jacket appeared in his hand. Tyler shrugged it on, then pulled the door closed behind him. He walked down the two front steps, passed me, and kept going.

"We'll talk in your car," he told me. "I won't have the entire neighborhood listening to my business."

The interior of the Volvo was only slightly warmer than the crisp air outside. As Tyler made himself comfortable in the passenger seat, I turned on the engine and blasted the heat.

"There's no need to warm the car on my account," he said. "I won't be here long. You need to understand that my mother is very ill. She doesn't have long to live."

"I'm sorry," I said.

"I don't want your condolences. What I want is for you to go away and leave us alone. Pete's descent into alcoholism was very distressing for my mother. His subsequent departure even more so."

"I understand that she and your brother were very close."

He closed his eyes briefly before speaking again.

"Yes, they were. Which is why she felt Pete's failures as a son, and a husband, and a father, all the more keenly. Though his disappearance came as a terrible shock, over time it also served to ease some of her turmoil. At least in his absence, Mother wasn't served a daily reminder of her son's deficiencies."

I stared at him across the seat. "Is that your mother's opinion or yours?"

"Let me tell you something, Ms. Travis. The only reason you and I are having this conversation is so I can make it clear that my brother's untimely demise is a topic Mother must be shielded from at all costs. Knowing what happened could only cause undue stress at a time when her life must remain as peaceful as possible."

"You didn't seem particularly upset by the news of your brother's death."

Tyler frowned "That's an unnecessarily personal observation. Not all families are happy ones, Ms. Travis."

He reached for the door handle. I was running out of time.

"Pete had started contacting people from his past, people he'd known in Stonebridge. I'm sure his family must have been at the top of that list." I finished what I wanted to say in a rush: "Pete got in touch with you, didn't he?"

Tyler's hand stilled. The car door remained closed.

"Not that it's any of your business," he said after a minute. "But yes, he and I spoke several weeks before he died. Pete tried to convince me that he'd stopped drinking. He told me he was putting his life in order."

"It was true," I said softly.

Tyler turned and looked at me. "Was it? If you truly believe that, you are a more gullible person than I. In the course of our conversation, Pete and I agreed on just one thing—that our mother's health and happiness was paramount. To let her hope that her older son had finally been restored to her, only to lose him once again to a relapse would have been tragic. A shock like that could have killed her."

I shook my head. "Maybe that should have been your mother's choice to make."

"No," Tyler said stubbornly. "Pete and I agreed. We made a deal. For once in his incurably selfish life, my brother put someone else's needs ahead of his own."

"What kind of deal?"

"If Pete stayed sober until the new year—if he managed to go a full four months without a drink—I would tell Mother that we had been in contact. Together she and I would welcome him home."

"But you never expected that to happen," I said.

"No, of course not. I was quite certain Pete wouldn't be able to uphold his end of the bargain." Tyler reached for the handle again. This time he pushed the door open before turning back to me. A draft of cold air came streaming into the warm car. "And as it turned out, I was right."

"Not entirely," I told him. "Pete's accident wasn't caused by alcohol. He wasn't drunk when he died."

Tyler's reaction wasn't what I'd expected. He merely shrugged.

"And yet the end result is still the same, isn't it? One way or another, Pete's reappearance in our lives would have had a devastating impact. You've only confirmed what I said from the beginning. I was right to remain silent. Good day, Ms. Travis. I hope we won't have occasion to meet again."

I'd have been tempted to slam the car door, but Tyler closed it softly behind him. Then he turned away from me and walked to his house. I watched until he went inside. Tyler never looked back.

Chapter
Fourteen

Wednesday afternoon after school, Sam was busy working and Davey, Kevin, and I were gathered around the kitchen table.

Davey, having summoned me to this get-together, had also supplied the refreshments. In front of each place setting was a mug of hot chocolate with pieces of candy cane floating on top. A plate of my favorite cinnamon Christmas cookies sat in the middle of the table. Next to my seat was a thick pad of lined paper accompanied by two pens.

Color me intrigued.

The Poodle pack, including honorary member Bud, had followed us out to the kitchen. As Davey, Kev, and I found our seats around the table the Poodles jostled for position on the floor.

Predictably, Tar flopped down beneath Kev's chair.

He was ever hopeful that food would drop into his mouth and Kevin was the most likely benefactor. Augie went straight to Davey. Faith and Eve lay down beside me. Raven and Bud curled up next to each other on the big dog bed tucked against the wall. Christmas music wafted through the room.

The stage was set. But for what?

"It's time to make Christmas lists," Davey announced.

Kev nodded his head in agreement. "It was my idea."

"Your idea?" Somehow that didn't come as a surprise. At almost-four, my younger son loved *everything* about Christmas. But still. "More lists? New lists? Additions to your previous lists?"

Kevin had begun to giggle. Davey was grinning too.

"I could have sworn you both gave me your Christmas lists before Thanksgiving." Seriously. They'd have handed them over before Halloween if I'd been receptive to the idea.

"They're not for *us*, silly," Kev informed me.

Davey waved a hand around the room. "They're for the Poodles."

"And Bud!" Kev added.

You know, in case there was any doubt. Which there hadn't been.

I gazed around at the canine corps. Now that we'd settled into our seats, most of the Poodles were snoozing contentedly. There was a basket of dog toys in the corner, but no one had opted to pull something out and start a game. Well-muscled, well-fed, with bright eyes and dense shiny coats, none of our dogs looked as though they lacked for anything.

Except perhaps for Tar, who was sadly lacking in brainpower. He'd flipped over on his back and was now lying with his tongue hanging out of his half-open mouth and all four feet pointing up in the air. Somehow I didn't think a Christmas list would help that.

"The Poodles have a stocking that we hang with all the others," I pointed out. "This year, Bud will be included. Do they *need* a list?"

I took a sip of my hot chocolate. It was rich and delicious. I had to hand it to Davey. The addition of crushed candy cane was pure genius.

"Everybody needs a Christmas list," he informed me. "Otherwise how will you know what to put in their stocking?"

"*Santa Claus* knows." I leveled Davey a warning look. "Santa Claus knows everything."

Kev frowned as he puzzled something through. Thankfully it wasn't Davey's gaffe. "If Santa knows everything, how come *we* made lists?"

"You guys were being helpful. Santa Claus is very busy this time of year."

"I know." Kevin nodded solemnly. "He was in the mall yesterday. Santa is everywhere."

"Kev was excited about making lists for the dogs," Davey said. "Wouldn't it be a good idea to be helpful on their behalf too?"

Put like that, what mother could possibly refuse?

I pulled over the pad of paper and uncapped one of the pens. "Okay. Who wants to start?"

"Me, me!" Kevin's hand shot up in the air. "The Poodles need biscuits and bones, and a new sock with a tennis ball in the toe because Augie threw the last one over the fence."

I looked up. "He did?"

"It was an accident," Davey said. "Tar was chasing him."

Oh. "What else?"

"Bud needs a winter coat," Kev told me. "Otherwise he's going to be cold in the snow."

"Bud has plenty of hair." I never dressed the Poodles up in clothing or costumes. Dogs in fashionable outfits just weren't my thing. "Plus, he lives in the house. He never has to stay outside if he doesn't want to."

"A coat," Kev repeated firmly. "Santa will understand. He lives in the North Pole. I bet his reindeer wear coats too."

"Bud is more likely to chew up a coat than wear it," I mentioned.

Kevin ignored me. "It should be plaid." He thought for a moment, then added, "Red and white with silver stars on it."

"Stars?" I repeated faintly. *Where was I going to find a plaid dog coat with stars on it?*

Davey was grinning again. He glanced at the paper in front of me. "Are you writing all that down?"

Kevin hopped up from his seat and came to have a look. He couldn't read yet, but he stared at the writing on the pad anyway. "Does that say *plaid*?" he asked. "It needs to say *plaid*."

PLAID, I wrote down in big block letters. WITH SILVER STARS.

I was pretty sure I was going to regret this.

Later that night, my cell phone rang. I didn't recognize the number. Everyone was gathered in the living room, watching Charlie Brown and Snoopy celebrate Christmas on TV. I carried the phone around the corner into the hall so I could hear.

"Is this Melanie?" a woman's voice asked. She sounded older and not entirely sure of herself. I wished she would speak up.

"Yes, it is. Who is this?"

"Stella Braverman. Do you remember me?"

I pressed the device closer to my ear. "Of course, Stella. How are you?"

"I'm well. Thank you for asking. But I need you to do something for me."

"Oh?"

"Well, not exactly for me. It's for my neighbor, Betty Dempsey. You've met her son, Tyler."

For a second, my breath caught. "Yes, I know who Betty Dempsey is. What does she need from me?"

"Betty wants to talk to you," Stella told me. "She wants to know what happened to Pete. She wants to hear it from you. In your own words."

"I'm not sure that's possible," I said. "Tyler has been very clear about the fact that he doesn't want me to see his mother. To be honest, I'm not even sure he's broken the news to her about Pete's death."

"No, he didn't. That coward." Stella's voice rose. "But I did. Betty deserved to know."

Good for her, I thought. Unfortunately that still didn't mean that I could do as she'd requested.

"I'm not sure how you expect me to get past Tyler," I said.

"Same way I do," Stella replied with a snort. "You wait until he's left the house, then you take my key and let yourself in."

"Stella, I live in Stamford. Even if you called me as soon as Tyler went out, by the time I got to Stonebridge, he could be back."

"That's why I set something up for tomorrow afternoon. Tyler's going to be called away between two and three o'clock. Can you make that?"

As plans went, it sounded far from perfect. There were a dozen questions I wanted to ask. And probably several good objections I should have made. But I realized immediately that this was likely to be my only chance to hear what Pete and Tyler's mother had to say about the rivalry between her two sons. And maybe to discover how far one of them might have gone to retain his place in the spotlight.

In reality, there was never any doubt about my reply.

"Yes," I said. "I can make that."

"*Again?*" Sam lifted a brow later the next morning when I informed him of my plans for the day.

"I suspect this will be my last visit to Stonebridge. I've already spoken to Pete's ex-wife, his business partners, his former best friend, his mistress, his brother, his neighbor, and even his high school girlfriend." I stopped and sighed. "You'd think I'd have an idea what caused Pete's death by now."

"Yes," Sam agreed drily. "You're usually quicker on the uptake. While you take another drive up the coast, the boys and I will be doing our bit and covering the office at the Christmas tree farm this afternoon. With Howard Academy having early dismissal on Fridays, I volunteered you to do the same tomorrow. I believe Aunt Peg intends to join you."

"Oh joy," I said. "She probably wants to spend the afternoon pumping me for information I don't possess."

Sam leaned down and brushed a kiss across the top of my head. "Maybe you'll learn something interesting today."

One could only hope, I thought.

Promptly at two o'clock, I pulled into Stella Braverman's driveway and coasted to a stop. Luckily the short strip of macadam was located on the opposite side of the house from the Dempsey home. Due to the clandestine nature of our business, I thought it wiser not to park on the street where the Volvo would be highly visible to passersby.

As I exited the car, Stella was already coming out her back door. She was dressed in furry boots and a hooded parka and had a determined look on her face. She was holding a key in her hand.

"Good, you're punctual," she said. "Let's go. I don't know how long Tyler's going to be gone. Trust me, it'll be better if he doesn't see us. Last time he caught me he tried to take my key away. Thank God Betty didn't let him, or we'd be out of luck today."

There was a well-worn path in the snow between the back of the two neighboring houses. Stella was spry for a woman her age and she obviously knew where she was going. I was happy to let her take the lead.

She elbowed aside a glass storm door, inserted her key in the lock, then shoved the inner door open. I followed her into a dark kitchen. As we paused to open our coats and wipe our boots on a thick fiber doormat, Stella reached over and turned on the lights.

"Betty?" she called out. "It's me and Melanie coming in the back door. We'll be right in to see you."

"Take your time, dear," a thin, reedy, voice called back. "I'm not going anywhere."

The living room opened directly off the kitchen. It too was only dimly lit. As we entered the room, a burst of light to one side drew my gaze. A television with its volume muted was showing what appeared to be an infomercial for cooking utensils.

"Turn that thing off, would you? The TV is nothing but an annoyance. I don't know why Tyler thinks it keeps me company." Betty Dempsey spoke up from the opposite side of the room.

A frail woman with gaunt features and wispy gray hair, she lay half-reclining on a low couch. The lower part of her body was covered by a light blanket and her head and shoulders were resting on a plump bank of pillows. She was staring at me with interest.

"You must be Melanie," Betty said. "Pleased to meet you. I hope you don't mind if I don't get up."

"Of course not. It's a pleasure to meet you too, Mrs. Dempsey." There was an upholstered chair beside the couch. I walked over and took a seat. When I leaned forward, the two of us were on the same level.

"I'll just give you ladies some time to get acquainted," Stella said. "If anybody needs me I'll be in the kitchen brewing some tea."

"I'm terribly sorry for your loss," I said.

Betty nodded somberly. "Thank you. My son's absence has been a hole in my life for these last years. In my condition, the only bright spot I have to look forward to is that I'll be seeing him again soon. I know you were there when he was found. Would you tell me what happened?"

I took my time relating the story, pausing for Betty to ask questions or add comments. I told her that Pete wouldn't have suffered. I mentioned that his best friend, Snowball, had been by his side at the end.

That part made Betty smile. She sat up and folded her hands together on the blanket. "That boy always did love animals. Back when he was young, Pete was always bringing home strays and nursing them back to health."

"What about Tyler?" I asked casually. "Did he like animals too?"

Betty's gaze narrowed. Her body might have been weak, but her perception hadn't dulled. "Stella has kept me apprised of your escapades around town. I'm sure you've already heard an earful about those two boys and how they treated one another. Now that I have nothing else to do but sit and think, I look back on it and I think maybe that was partly my fault."

She paused and drew in a deep breath. One hand fluttered upward. She placed it over her heart. "Pete's birth was the answer to many prayers. I'd had two miscarriages before he arrived. The doctors weren't sure I'd ever be able to carry a baby to term. My husband and I called him our little miracle."

It was easy to imagine that Tyler would have found that a hard act to follow.

"When Pete's drinking spiraled out of control it ruined my life too." Betty's voice was growing fainter. I hoped my visit wasn't tiring her out. "That boy had every opportunity handed to him and he threw it all away. When I was diagnosed, I asked Tyler to try and find his brother. Did he tell you that?"

I nodded in silence. Unexpected tears pricked the corners of my eyes. I had no desire to cover up Tyler's misdeeds but I couldn't break this woman's heart by telling her that shortly before his death, Pete had wanted to come home. And her younger son had prevented him from doing so.

"Tyler thinks he needs to protect me," Betty said softly. "He's wrong about that, but he never listens. His father was the same way. He tried to shield me from things he thought I was better off not knowing. But of course I knew anyway. I've always known. I could see what was right in front of me."

She leaned back and rested her head on the pillows. Her gaze grew misty. I had no idea what Betty was talking about. Or if indeed, she was still talking to me at all. She seemed to be lost in a reminiscence of times past.

"What was right in front of you?" I asked.

"Life," Betty whispered. "Beautiful, miraculous life. A little girl with hazel eyes just like Pete's, who I never had a chance to know. I should have spoken up, but instead I let time pass. Then it was too late and I had to watch her grow up from afar. Pete should have made things right. That I allowed him not to will always be my biggest regret."

As she was speaking, Betty's lips curved in a small smile. I wondered if she was picturing a little girl with hazel eyes.

"I wasn't aware the Pete and Penny had a daughter," I said.

"They don't," Stella said from behind me. She walked into the room carrying a tea tray. "Betty, how about a nice, warm cup of tea?"

Betty blinked several times before focusing her gaze on her friend. "That would be lovely. Will you pour?"

I turned to Stella. "Betty was just talking about—"

"It's time for tea," Stella said. "Then we'll have to go. We wouldn't want anything about our visit to upset Betty."

"No, of course not," I agreed.

The tea was quickly poured and drunk. Fifteen minutes later, we'd said our good-byes and Stella had locked the door to the Dempsey home behind us.

"You'd better be on your way," she told me when we reached her driveway. "We don't want Tyler to come home and find you here."

Stella kept walking toward her house. I stopped beside my car.

"Betty was telling me about a little girl," I said.

Stella paused and looked back. "Betty's on a lot of medication these days. Sometimes her thoughts wander. I'm sure it wasn't anything important."

I didn't believe that for a minute. In fact, I was pretty sure that the opposite was true. It seemed to me that Betty's memories might be more significant than anything else I'd learned thus far. Now I had to figure out how to make that nugget of information fit with everything else I knew.

On the drive home, I realized the answer was easy. I'd dump everything in Aunt Peg's lap and let her make sense of it. Friday afternoon at Haney's Holiday Home was going to be interesting indeed.

Chapter
Fifteen

When Aunt Peg blew into the office at the Christmas tree farm the following afternoon, Faith and I were waiting for her.

She was carrying Snowball under her arm and moving with the determined stride of a woman on a mission. It was no wonder Aunt Peg wasn't walking the silky-haired Maltese on a leash. He probably wouldn't have been able to keep up.

"*Well!*" She stopped in front of me and propped her free hand on her hip. "It's about time."

It was a good thing there weren't any customers in the office right then. Anyone with an ounce of sense would have taken one look at the expression on Aunt Peg's face and run for the hills.

Which said nothing for the quality of my brain cells, because instead I stood my ground, grinned in the face of her obvious wrath, and said, "Time for what?"

Aunt Peg snorted indelicately. She set Snowball down on the plank floor, then unzipped her parka, pulled it off, and tossed it behind the counter. Her scarf and hat followed. Then she turned back to me.

"Is your phone working?"

"I believe so."

"Can you make calls with it? Send an e-mail? Maybe a text?"

"All possibilities," I confirmed.

Aunt Peg gazed at Faith who was lying beside the woodstove, and shook her head sadly. Faith flapped her tail up and down in support. "Then for heaven's sake, what is *wrong* with you? It's been how long since we spoke . . . a month?"

"Actually less than a week—"

"Indeed the silence on your end had become *so* deafening I'd begun to look for smoke signals."

"Now that's just silly," I said.

"You wouldn't think so if you were in my shoes. Thank goodness for Snowball. Otherwise I'd have been entirely lacking in suitable companionship."

"I'm going to tell your Poodles you said that," I mentioned.

Snowball came bounding out from behind the counter. He had his teeth fastened on the end of Aunt Peg's wool scarf and was dragging it along the floor behind him. As the Maltese went racing by, I leaned down and scooped him up. The scarf came with him.

It took a minute to pry the two apart. By the time I'd succeeded in doing so, Aunt Peg seemed to have settled. She sat down in the rocking chair. I walked over and deposited Snowball in her lap. I'd just reached down to give Faith a pat when the door opened again and a family of four—two smiling adults and two exuberant children—came inside.

Most of the customers I'd dealt with so far were old hands at locating and chopping down their own trees. Many had brought the tools they'd need to do the job with them. This family was similarly prepared. All I had to do was hand out candy canes, show them where the sleds were waiting by the side of the building, and point them in the direction of the Christmas tree forest.

In the brief lull that followed, I quickly told Aunt Peg about my visit with Betty Dempsey the previous afternoon. She sat and mulled that over while I dealt with two more sets of customers, one who needed help getting their tree tied to the roof of their car, and a second who wanted to negotiate a price for the inflatable Santa Claus—a decoration that wasn't for sale.

"Are you thinking what I'm thinking?" she asked when we again had the cozy office to ourselves.

I lifted a brow and waited. Before voicing my suspicions, I wanted to hear what Aunt Peg had to say. As usual, she didn't disappoint.

"It sounds to me as though the little girl whom she watched from afar might be Betty's grandchild."

"I agree," I said. "And there's more."

This time I backtracked to my conversation with Pete's ex-mistress, Olivia, about her former lover's demons. After that, we got sidetracked when I mentioned Rufus the Great Dane. Somewhat predictably that led to a discussion of Aunt Peg's aversion to dog parks.

Customers came inside to pay for a tree they'd picked out and when they left, I once again picked up the thread of my story. I'd now worked my way around to Pete's high school sweetheart, Sharon LaRue. By this time, Aunt Peg was sitting up straighter in her seat. Considering the state of the rocking chair, that wasn't an easy feat.

"There was a photograph on Sharon's desk," I said.

"Let me guess." She placed Snowball on the floor and stood up. "Was it a little girl with hazel eyes?"

"Not quite," I admitted. "It showed her husband and a grown-up daughter whose eye color I didn't bother to notice at the time. Sharon told me that she and her husband had married when they were very young. During their freshman year of college, in fact."

"I'd say that's rather interesting timing." Aunt Peg walked over to the window in the back wall. She stared at the forest thoughtfully. Though it was only mid-afternoon, we were close to the shortest day of the year. The sun was already dropping in the sky. "What did she have to say about Pete's high school peccadilloes?"

"She told me that Pete's only problem back then was his rivalry with his brother. That if there were unresolved issues in his life, they'd have had to do with his family."

Aunt Peg glanced at me over her shoulder. "And you believed her?"

"At the time I had no reason not to. But now . . ."

"You're wondering," Aunt Peg said. "As am I."

At that moment, the happy family of four returned to pay for their tree and to browse through our selection of Christmas ornaments. Twenty minutes passed before I was able to get back to Aunt Peg. In the meantime, she'd wandered outside and helped another family wrangle their tree from sled to vehicle. As I stepped out onto the porch to check on their progress, I realized how dark it had grown and turned on all the outdoor lights.

The area surrounding the office and its outbuilding was well-lit but the dense woods were not. Frank had asked me to stay open until five o'clock, but I doubted we'd see any additional shoppers that afternoon.

Aunt Peg and I made short work of checking out the last tree buyers. As their vehicles' taillights disappeared down the driveway, all appeared quiet. I closed the office door firmly to keep the warmth inside.

"It looks as though we're done for the day," Aunt Peg said with satisfaction. "Let's get back to what really matters. What else do you have to tell me?"

"One last thing. John Smith said that Pete had been contacting people he'd wronged in the past."

"I know that. I was there." She flicked a hand impatiently, waving me on.

"Several people I spoke with in Stonebridge told me that they'd heard from him. But not Sharon. She was adamant about the fact that they hadn't been in touch in years."

"Maybe he hadn't worked his way around to her yet," Aunt Peg said dubiously.

I didn't believe that. I was pretty sure Aunt Peg didn't either.

"Or maybe she was one of the first people he contacted," I said. "And she was lying to cover up the fact that she knew exactly what Pete was doing and where to find him."

Aunt Peg was nodding as I spoke. Now she said, "That information needs to go to the police. Those new details added to the autopsy result ought to be enough to convince them that their initial conclusion about Pete's death was incorrect."

If not, her tone implied, she would browbeat the officers in charge until they changed their minds.

"You and I can go together tomorrow morning," I said.

"Excellent." Aunt Peg picked up her scarf and wrapped it around her neck. "Now that we have that settled, Snowball and I are going to take a walk. I've discovered that caretakers of small dogs must adapt to the needs of their tiny bladders. Are the lights on out back?"

"Yes, I turned everything on a few minutes ago. While you do that, I'll close the cash register. Then we can all leave together."

Faith elected to stay inside the warm office with me. She watched as I counted the day's receipts, and then I tucked them into a bank pouch that went in a small safe beneath the counter. I was leaning down and fiddling with the combination when a blast of cold air signaled that the door had opened once again. Aunt Peg and Snowball were back sooner than I'd expected.

Then I heard the rumble of a low growl from Faith and quickly readjusted my thinking. The big Poodle had been greeting incoming strangers with warmth and equanimity all afternoon. But whoever had entered the office now clearly did not meet with her approval.

Slowly I rose to my feet. Sharon LaRue was standing in the doorway.

"Oh," I said, surprised. "What are you doing here?"

Sharon nudged the door shut with her foot. "We need to talk. What's the matter with your dog?"

I glanced at Faith. "Nothing. She's fine."

"She's not fine. She's growling." Sharon still hadn't advanced into the small room. "I can hear it. Does she bite?"

"Only people she doesn't like."

Faith probably rolled her eyes at that, but I didn't look over to check. The Poodle's instincts were always spot-on. If there was something about our unexpected visitor she didn't like, I was willing to trust her response. I remained behind the counter and I kept my gaze firmly fixed on Sharon.

"How did you find me here?" I asked. I wasn't aware that she and I had ever discussed my connection to the Christmas tree farm.

"I had dinner last night with my Aunt Stella. She had several interesting things to tell me."

Aunt Stella. My breath jammed in my throat.

What an idiot I was. I'd overlooked one of the chief characteristics of small, insular towns. One way or another, almost everybody had a connection to everyone else.

"She told me you went to see Betty Dempsey yesterday."

"That's right. Betty asked to see me. She wanted to talk to me about Pete's death."

"I heard that's not all you and she discussed."

Hand held low, I gave my fingers a soft snap. Faith padded quietly around the counter to my side. Once there, she pressed her body against my leg. Clearly, she was still uneasy. And because of that, so was I.

Sharon could no longer see Faith, but she still didn't step away from the door. That was just as well. The office was a small space. Even standing on the other side of the room, the other woman still felt uncomfortably close.

Sharon wasn't looking at me, however. Instead her gaze was sliding dismissively over the colorful jumble of holiday decorations that Claire had hung on the walls. "Geez, what were you thinking when you put up all this crap? It looked like the North Pole exploded in here."

Affronted on Claire's behalf, I said, "Did you come here to discuss the décor?"

"No, I came to tell to you to stop sticking your nose into everybody's business." Her eyes returned to me. "Betty's an old lady. She's sick. Sometimes she doesn't know what she's saying."

"Betty seemed perfectly lucid to me." That might have been a stretch, but I went with it anyway.

"That's not for you to judge. You don't even know the Dempseys."

"You're right," I agreed mildly. "I couldn't possibly know them as well as someone like you who's been friends with them for years." I paused a beat, then added, "Or possibly more than friends."

Sharon still hadn't unbuttoned her coat. Or taken off her hat. She wasn't wearing gloves and now she shoved her hands deep into her pockets. She glared at me angrily.

"You want to talk about Pete?" she snapped. "Fine, let's do that. Pete Dempsey was a spoiled, selfish, rotten excuse for a human being and I'm glad he's dead."

"Did you kill him?" I asked.

"Not me. The booze did that."

"Pete hadn't been drinking when he died," I told her. "He didn't freeze to death because he collapsed in a drunken stupor. He died because someone hit him over the head with a tree branch and left him lying in the snow."

Sharon scowled. "Don't look at me like you think I ought to be sorry about that. Nobody in Stonebridge is sorry. Pete's death wasn't a loss to any of us. When he left town, we were all happy to see him go."

"But that was the problem, wasn't it?" I prodded gently. "Pete was coming back. He'd gotten sober and he'd been contacting people from his past. You told me you hadn't heard from him in years, but I think you lied about that. I'm guessing you were one of the first people he called."

"No, that's not true." Sharon's deep chuckle had an ugly edge. "I *should* have been the first person Pete apologized to. But I wasn't. He took his own sweet time getting around to me."

She shook her head as if she could hardly believe it. "And even then—when he was trying to make me believe he wanted to be a better man—Pete still couldn't admit that what he'd done to me was wrong. He had the nerve to say that my life turned out fine in the end, so what right did I have to be upset with him?"

"Wow." I winced. "That would have pissed me off too."

"I know. *Right?*"

For a brief moment Sharon and I were in perfect agreement. Then I spoiled our accord by saying, "You were pregnant at the end of your senior year of high school, weren't you? Is Pete Amy's father?"

Sharon didn't reply to my question directly. Instead she said, "I was only eighteen years old. I had no idea which way to turn. When I told Pete, he said, 'That's your problem. You find a way to deal with it.' Then he left for college."

I didn't want to feel sympathy for her, but hearing her story I almost couldn't help it. "In your place, I'd have been furious," I said.

"Fury was a luxury I didn't have time for," Sharon snapped. "Steve and I were married six weeks later."

"Did he know?"

"Not right away. But later on, yes. He and I have a great relationship. We had our issues in the beginning, but we worked through them."

Issues indeed, I thought. How great could a relationship be when it was founded upon a lie?

Sharon thrust out her chin. "Steve loves Amy. In every way that matters, he *is* her father."

Something—a spark of apprehension—flashed in her eyes. Right then I knew: Steve wasn't the one who was the problem.

"Amy doesn't know who her real father is, does she?"

"No, of course not. Why would I have told her something like that? My daughter doesn't need to know that her father is a lying, cheating, bastard who abandoned me as soon as he found out she existed."

"Pete wanted to tell her the truth, didn't he?" I was guessing, but the anguished expression on Sharon's face confirmed that I was right.

"There was no way I could let him do that," she

said. "I wasn't about to let Pete ruin Amy's life the way he ruined mine. He refused to claim her back then. It was too late for him to want to be her father now."

"I agree," I said.

Casually I stepped out from behind the counter, like we were just two women having a perfectly normal conversation. Earlier I'd left my phone near the woodstove. As Sharon continued to speak, I slid my gaze that way.

"I had no choice but to protect Amy." Her voice rose with the conviction that she'd been right. "Amy was *mine*. Not his. But Pete refused to accept that he'd lost any right to his daughter twenty-three years ago when he walked out on me. I wasn't about to let that scumbag come back and dismantle the life I'd built for myself."

"What did you do?" I asked, inching toward the back of the room.

"I told Pete he could take his stupid atonement ritual and shove it. His reappearance would have destroyed Amy and *for what*? To make himself feel better? That was never going to happen. Not while there was a single breath left in my body."

It was a chilling statement of intent. I heard Faith whimper softly under her breath. It was almost as if she knew what was coming.

"So now you know why I've come." Sharon's lips flattened into a hard line. "I have to protect my family. The story I told you ends here, today, with you and me."

She withdrew her hand from her pocket. It was holding a gun. Sharon lifted it and pointed it at me. "Stop right there, Melanie. Don't move."

Chapter
Sixteen

I froze in place and held up a hand. *As if that would help.* "Wait. Let's talk about this."

"I have nothing more to say. Except maybe that I'm sorry it's come to this." Sharon looked at me across the short expanse. "Although it's your own fault."

"It hasn't come to anything yet," I said quickly.

There was no way I could get to my phone. I cast my gaze around the room, searching for a weapon. The only thing I saw was a thick piece of firewood. That would be ironic.

"How did you do it?" I asked, stalling for time. With the barrel of a gun pointed at my midsection, what choice did I have?

"It wasn't hard," Sharon said dismissively. "After I got over the shock of hearing from Pete, I told him that I wanted to meet with him in person. But not in Stonebridge. I insisted on coming to him."

"And he was all right with that?" I asked, surprised. I wouldn't have thought Pete would want his old friends to see how he was living.

"It wasn't as if I gave him a choice. Pete knew the only way he could get to Amy was by going through me. I told him if I was satisfied with our conversation, I would let him talk to her."

"But you never had any intention of doing so," I said.

"Of course not." Sharon looked at me like I was daft. "We met outside this building. This place was deserted then. Pete was all alone out here in the middle of nowhere."

She must have initially gotten together with Pete after Mr. Haney died and before Frank purchased the property. The Christmas tree farm would have been closed then. And empty.

"I asked Pete to show me where he lived and he did." Sharon shuddered. "It was disgusting. I couldn't believe he'd sunk that low. After I saw that, all I had to do was go home and come up with a plan."

"It was a good plan," I told her. "Pete's death appeared to be an accident."

"That was the idea." Sharon sounded smug. "I decided to show up with a couple bottles of gin and get Pete so drunk that he passed out. After that, it would be easy enough to turn off the dinky little stove and leave him there in the cold." She stopped and frowned.

"But Pete refused to cooperate. Considering our past history, maybe I should have expected that."

Yeah maybe, I thought. "Then what did you do?"

"I told Pete I wanted to go for a moonlight walk in the snow with him. And he fell for it. Can you believe it?"

I shook my head. Honestly, I couldn't. The male ego was a wondrous thing.

"I took one of the liquor bottles with me. I was sure that when he got chilly enough, I could convince him to warm up with a drink. But then I saw that branch just lying on the ground. It was perfect, like fate had placed it there for me. Once I hit him over the head, Mother Nature did the rest."

"Presumably except for dumping the gin on him and leaving the empty bottles in his cabin," I said drily.

"Yes, except for that." My sarcasm had gone right over her head.

"You fooled the police last time," I said. "But they'll be suspicious about a second death here. If you shoot me with your gun, you're not going to be able to explain that away."

"That won't be a problem." Sharon sounded remarkably sure of herself. "The police will think this was a robbery gone bad. Probably kids looking for drug money. A remote location and a woman alone with a cash register? It's the perfect setup."

Damn, I thought. *She was right*. Except for one thing. I wasn't alone. Apparently Sharon didn't realize that.

"Plus," she added, "you don't strike me as the kind of person who would meekly hand over the cash to stay safe. Probably everybody knows what a pain in the butt you can be."

Well, okay. She might be right. But that meant I wasn't about to let her meekly shoot me either. Not if I could figure out a way to stop her.

Faith was still making low noises. Her whimper had turned into an angry whine. She didn't know a thing about guns but she must have felt the palpable edge of menace in the air. The Poodle came out from behind the counter on her toes with her shoulders arched. The hair on her neck and shoulders was standing straight up.

"Don't even think of siccing that dog on me." Sharon cut Faith a glance. "If you do, I'll shoot her first."

I cupped my hand around Faith's muzzle and quickly maneuvered her around behind me. "Nobody's going to be shooting anybody."

"I wouldn't bet on that if I were you."

From somewhere outside, there came a blood-curdling scream. At the same moment the door to the office came flying inward.

The solid wooden panel hit Sharon hard from behind, catching her squarely across the shoulders. She stumbled and went staggering forward. Her arms flailed in the air as she tried to regain her balance. It didn't happen.

I briefly registered the panicked look on Sharon's face before whirling around to grab Faith. As Sharon fell, her finger tightened on the trigger. With a roar that sounded impossibly loud in the small space, the gun discharged.

Faith and I hit the floor together. I was on top, and the big dog cushioned my frantic dive without complaint. I heard the sound of a loud pop. To my surprise, it was followed by the whoosh of escaping air.

I'd started to raise my head, but immediately ducked down again as something red and white went flying past us. I was still trying to process that when the unidentified missile suddenly shot upward. Several large splinters of wood came raining down from the cabin ceiling. A loud plop followed.

Quickly I disengaged myself from Faith and scrambled to my feet. Right now, there wasn't time to think about anything but getting to the gun.

Sharon had dropped the weapon when she'd used her hands to break her fall, but she was already looking around for it. From my vantage point I could see that the gun had skidded across the floor and come to rest beside the counter. I went racing after it, but I didn't get there first.

Aunt Peg beat me to it.

She crossed the room in four quick strides and

scooped up the gun, handling the piece with the calm assurance of someone who was accustomed to riding to the rescue. Then she spun around and trained the weapon on Sharon, who'd risen slowly to her knees.

"I don't think so," Aunt Peg said.

"Who the hell are you?" Sharon spat out. She dusted off her hands and started to get up.

"You may think of me as the cavalry," Aunt Peg said with a wolfish smile. "The police are on their way. I'd rather you remain on the floor until they arrive. I'd hate to have to use this, but I will if I need to."

Sharon grimaced as though her knees were hurting, but she lowered herself back down on the wooden planking. A small, mean part of me was gratified to see that she appeared to be in pain. Having threatened to shoot us, Sharon was getting off easy, in my book.

On the other side of the room, Faith was up and moving well. She'd trotted over to the far corner and was busy examining something crumpled on the floor. Satisfied that she was in good shape, I turned to Aunt Peg.

"That was a rash move," I said.

"But effective. At least you might credit me that."

"The shot went wild," I pointed out. "You could have gotten me killed."

Aunt Peg just shrugged. *All's well that ends well.*

It was easy for her to be so blithe about it. There hadn't been a gun pointed in her direction. Meanwhile the aftershock of my near miss had left me feeling unaccountably grumpy.

"It took you long enough to make your move," I said.

"I was listening to what Sharon had to say." Aunt Peg flicked a quick glance my way. "After all, it's not as though you've gone out of your way to keep me apprised."

"You could hear us from outside?"

"Of course. I was on the porch. This old building is hardly soundproof. Those wooden walls have gaps wider than my little finger."

I took a sudden look around. "Wait a minute. Where's Snowball?"

"Don't worry about him, he's safe in my van. I stashed him there when I rounded the building and saw Sharon's car. I thought perhaps I might need to have my wits about me. It's a good thing I'd done so, because when I heard her threaten Faith, I knew I had to intervene."

"When you heard her threaten *Faith*?" As I recalled, that had happened a good minute after Sharon had threatened to shoot *me*.

"Precisely." Aunt Peg nodded. "That's when I knew things were about to get serious."

I opened my mouth. Then shut it again. Upon reflection, there was absolutely nothing I could say to that. Instead I went to check on Faith.

She was still in the corner, sniffing at something.

From afar, it looked like a discarded bundle of clothing. But when I nudged the Poodle aside and took a closer look, the object of her curiosity turned out to be the remains of our inflatable Santa Claus. The bullet Sharon fired had missed both Faith and me, but it had struck Santa directly in the middle of his red vinyl chest.

The cheery, life-size, holiday figure was a goner. Under the circumstances, it seemed like a small price to pay.

Chapter
Seventeen

"**D**o you hear something?" Aunt Peg asked. She lifted a hand to her ear.

Sirens. A minute later, the still-open doorway revealed several sets of flashing lights coming closer through the trees.

Hopefully it was just my imagination that Aunt Peg appeared to surrender the gun with reluctance when the first police officers came through the door. She was enough of a menace when she wasn't holding a weapon. I hated to think that she might be developing a fondness for firearms.

Aunt Peg and I took turns explaining the situation to the responding officers while Sharon listened in stony silence. Her gun and the demolished Santa Claus were enough to get her taken into custody. In addition, the officers promised to pass along what we told them about Pete Dempsey's death to their superiors.

Sharon immediately hired a lawyer. Thanks to his quick work, she was out of jail the next day. I couldn't help but wonder what kind of reception she would receive from the good folks of Stonebridge upon her return to town.

Later I heard from Aunt Peg—who followed each new development avidly—that Sharon's attorney was discussing such things as mitigating circumstances and a conspicuous lack of hard evidence with the DA. Apparently, the blameless life the assistant principal had led thus far would also work in her favor.

Now that the police and the courts were handling things, I put that adventure behind me and threw myself into preparations for Christmas. *Better late, than never.* Once the upcoming holiday finally had my full attention, it all came together beautifully.

On Christmas morning, everything was perfect. Or as near to perfect as things could ever be in a family with one child starry-eyed over Santa's visit, a teenager and five Standard Poodles who were all too clever for their own good, a semi-trained mutt, and two adults who had resigned themselves to living in a constant state of near-lunacy.

Of course we were awake early on Christmas morning. That was a given. Several inches of new snow had turned the outdoors fresh and white overnight. When we lit a fire in the fireplace and turned on the Christmas tree lights, the entire living room glowed.

The boys tore into their presents, greeting each new

gift with appreciation, even the clothing and books. When Kevin reached for a small box that was tucked way back beneath the tree, Sam and I shared a private smile.

"What do you suppose that is?" Sam asked.

Kev held up the box and shook it, like he'd seen his brother do.

"That sounds like more clothes," Davey predicted. He was busy examining a new wireless controller with thumb sticks.

"I hope it's not socks," Kevin said seriously. "I have lots of those."

"I don't think Santa brought you socks," I told him. "Open it and see."

Kevin yanked off the bow and opened the box. A peanut butter dog biscuit was sitting on top of a bed of tissue paper. He frowned, perplexed. "Why did Santa bring me a dog biscuit?"

"Maybe it goes with what's underneath," Sam said. "Keep looking."

Davey stopped what he was doing to watch too. So we were all paying attention when Kevin pushed aside the tissue wrapping and began to shriek. Jumping to his feet, he held up a red plaid dog coat decorated across the back with a spray of silver stars.

"Santa brought it!" Kevin exclaimed. "I knew he would."

Sam had gone from store to store until he'd found the perfect chew-resistant jacket. Meanwhile I'd bought a length of silver fabric and made stars. I'd spent the last several nights, after the boys were in bed, sewing them on. The look on Kevin's face when he'd opened the present made the extra effort well worth it.

Bud was immediately brought forward and buckled into his new coat. The little dog stood in place for a few seconds, whipping his head from side to side to examine his new outfit. Then he leapt away and began to race around the room.

As Kevin cheered and the Poodles watched in bemused wonderment, Bud shot across the living room floor and gave a sudden flying leap that landed him on the couch. From there, he hopped to a nearby chair, then skimmed across a tabletop before landing on the floor again.

He was about to repeat the circuit of the room when Sam stepped in and scooped him up. "I think we'd better let them take this game outside before the Poodles decide to join in the festivities and they wreck the place."

Great idea.

Aunt Peg showed up when we were seated at the kitchen table, eating a Christmas breakfast of French toast and slab-cut bacon. Having gone directly from presents to food, we were all still in our jammies. I was surprised Aunt Peg was out and about so early on Christmas.

"I needed to make an early holiday delivery," she explained as she joined us and helped herself to a plate of food. "Snowball has gone off to his new home."

"On Christmas morning?"

We were all aware of Aunt Peg's firm objection to puppies being given as presents on the busy holiday. That she would even consider participating in such a scheme herself came as a shock. Aunt Peg, however, remained unruffled.

She slid another slice of bacon onto her plate and said, "It took this long to get things settled, since nobody seemed to know precisely who Snowball belonged to. Not surprisingly, Pete didn't leave a will. So I took myself over to Stonebridge and talked to his family. They didn't want anything to do with the poor little dog."

I lifted my head in surprise. "You spoke with *Tyler?*"

"Of course. You're not the only one around here who gets to ask questions. I talked to Betty too. She asked me if I might be able to find Snowball a good home. So that's precisely what I did."

"But still," said Sam. "Christmas morning?"

"This was a special case. The Butlers are a retired couple. Their children are grown and have families of their own. This year no one was making the trip home for the holiday. So Ned and Sally would be spending a quiet day by themselves."

I gazed around our lively table crowded with loved

ones. I couldn't help but feel sorry for anyone who had to spend the holidays alone.

"I'd extended some feelers in the Maltese community," Aunt Peg continued. "Their local rescue put me in touch with Ned. Apparently he'd proposed to Sally forty years ago on Christmas Day, and sealed the deal with a Maltese puppy. They'd been dog owners ever since, until they lost their last pet three months ago."

"That's sad," said Kevin. The rest of us nodded.

"Recently Sally had indicated to Ned that she might be ready to open her heart to a new dog. At their age, she thought an adult dog might suit better than a puppy. So Ned contacted the local Maltese club. He and I spoke on the phone, then he came and met Snowball. The two of them hit it off beautifully. Ned wanted to surprise his wife on Christmas morning and, under the circumstances, I was happy to oblige."

"That was a very nice thing you did," Sam said softly.

I couldn't seem to talk past the lump in my throat, so I just nodded again. Even Davey looked subdued. Not Kevin. He was shaking his head.

"Ned should have asked Santa Claus for a dog," he said with impeccable three-year-old logic. "Santa would have brought him one."

I reached over and ruffled my son's hair. "But this way Snowball got a great home. And with Aunt Peg helping out, Santa had more time to spend making children happy."

"Oh." Kev considered that. The thought of Santa Claus working hard on his behalf made him smile. "Well done, Aunt Peg."

Well done, indeed.

MELANIE'S FAVORITE CINNAMON COOKIES

These cookies are great for busy moms. They're delicious and easy to make, and most people already have the ingredients in the pantry. Enjoy!

Ingredients
1¼ cup of butter
⅔ cup of sugar
⅓ cup brown sugar
1 egg yolk
1¼ cup of flour
1¼ teaspoons cinnamon
¼ teaspoon salt

Preheat your oven to 300 degrees.

Mix the butter, the sugar, and the brown sugar.

Add the egg yolk and blend well.

Stir together the flour, cinnamon, and salt. Add the dry ingredients to the creamed mixture and blend well.

Place the dough by rounded teaspoons on an ungreased cookie sheet. Bake for 20–25 minutes. Cool on the cookie sheet for a few minutes, then transfer to wax paper or a wire rack to finish cooling.

Yield: about 3 dozen cookies (unless you make each cookie twice as big as it should be like I do, in which case you will have half that many.)